SIREN STORIES

Presents

WHAT IVY WANTS

A Novel

J.J. Barnes

This book is dedicated to my mother, Elizabeth Albright, who has had my back every day of my life, and who took off her earrings during my divorce.

Chapter One

Ivy Rhodes plucked a cream-filled chocolate out of the box on her desk. She examined it glumly then bit into it. Given the circumstances it tasted exactly as it should. Not terrible, but somewhat disappointing.

There was a quiet coughing noise from her right. She turned and saw Helen, the slightly too nosy but perfectly friendly woman in the cubicle to her left, observing her with a hopeful look in her eye.

"Would you like a chocolate?" Ivy offered.

"Oh, go on," said Helen, shuffling her wheely desk chair across the aisle towards her. "If you insist."

Helen happily took a chocolate and pushed it into her mouth, making that fake orgasm face that always made Ivy feel a little bit violated. Given how disappointing the chocolates actually were, she felt like she was getting more insight into Helen and her husband's relationship than was strictly appropriate.

"How's your birthday going?" Helen asked her, once the orgasm-inducing chocolate had been swallowed.

Ivy shrugged. She was expected to enthuse about lovely gifts and romantic gestures, so that Helen could feel satisfied that her social duty had been performed adequately, but she couldn't quite muster anything beyond, "Pretty good."

Honestly, it hadn't started well. Ivy always looked forward to her birthday, and Steven always made a big fuss of her, but today he'd been so distracted by a work issue that had been plaguing him for a few days that he'd forgotten to make the traditional breakfast in bed she always looked forward to. Ivy had lain in bed all eager, waiting for the smell of bacon to waft through, before getting up and finding him shoving things into a bag and pulling on his coat.

"Morning," she had said tentatively.

He had laid a flat kiss on her cheek before hurrying out of the door and vanishing without speaking a word to her, leaving Ivy standing there in her pyjamas feeling thoroughly forgotten.

"Doing anything nice later?" asked Helen, helping herself to a second chocolate, and smiling warmly at Ivy with a twinkle in her eye.

Fuck's sake. Social duty performed, Helen. Take your chocolate and go!

"Steven's planning a romantic dinner," she said, smiling and nodding. At least that was something genuinely good. She wanted to dress up in a sexy little dress, forget she was thirty years old now, and have a wonderful evening eating, drinking, and laughing with her handsome husband.

"Nice," said Helen, nodding in approval, before scooting away back to her desk.

Ivy turned back to her computer, ready to crack on with the riveting world of hot tub sales. Eurgh! She was thirty years old. How could she be thirty years old and STILL stuck in this stupid job she'd only applied for in the first place because she needed a short-term financial fix. All these years later... here she sat. Same chair. Same office.

She grumpily shoved another chocolate into her mouth. Of course, it would be the orange one. She made full ick face as she tried to get it chewed up fast, then chugged some coffee to wash it away.

"What a face!" came a laughing voice from above her.

Ivy glared upwards. Tom from HR, one of the more irritating men in the office, was standing over her desk, leaning on the partition like he owned it, and plucking a fairy cake out of the basket she had dumped there on arrival.

Ivy smiled up at him as politely as she could possibly muster as he leered down at her with eyebrows raised. She shifted carefully and did the top button of her cardigan up.

"Happy birthday, love," he said, with a wink.

"Thanks, petal," said Ivy. *Honestly, what a sleaze.*

Tom blinked, a little confused by the strange greeting, but the smiled amiably. "Having a nice day, are we?"

Before Ivy was forced to take the conversation further, the phone on her desk rang. Ivy made an apologetic gesture then picked up the phone and turning her chair away from Tom.

"Ivy Rhodes, sales department."

"Ivy Rhodes!" came the voice of her boss. "Hugh here. Can you pop into my office for a quick word?"

Ivy closed her eyes for a second before reapplying her sales smile. "Absolutely, I can," she said, forcing bright enthusiasm into her voice as she cranked out the phrase she had perfected for faking positivity in her first week. "I'll be right there!"

Being called into the boss' office on her birthday could only be for something nice. Hugh loved a birthday. His own, more than anything, but birthdays in general were always a high point in his otherwise dull, beige week. He was probably waiting to present her with some swanky gift, and she could endure Hugh Bright for the fun of a swanky gift. Of course, he'd probably come in for a hug after she'd opened it... but still.

Ivy stood up and headed across the room towards Hugh's office. "Good luck," said Helen.

"Cheers," said Ivy, smiling a grimace at her. Hugh's hugs were legendary. Her best friend Julia had advised reporting him and her other best friend Mya had advised punching him swiftly in the penis. Ivy had opted for a polite avoidance and had perfected the Christmas party mistletoe swerve. She'd never been good at confrontation and hated causing a fuss.

"Ivy Rhodes," said Hugh as Ivy entered, his arms wide as though inflicting the hug on her from across the room before she'd even got into the office properly. "How the devil are you?"

"Fine, thanks," she said, stepping into the office.

"Pop the door closed there, would you?" he said, standing up from behind his desk and coming round to the front.

Ivy pushed the door closed as Hugh perched on the edge of his desk and attempted to cross one leg over the other in a nonchalant way before wobbling and giving up on the pose.

"Take a seat," he said.

Ivy glanced around as she sat. No gift... perhaps it was in an envelope? Envelopes were good.

"So," said Hugh, folding his arms. "The big three-oh, eh?"

"Yes," said Ivy, trying to sound happy about it. If she sounded even the slightest bit bothered by her age, he might tease her. She was in no mood to be teased. "That's right!"

In truth it did bother her. It bothered her deep in her core. Not the age itself- she wasn't upset about growing older exactly. Her grandmother had always told her that growing old was a privilege not everybody was afforded and should be treated as such. No, it wasn't the actual age... it was what she'd done with the years prior to it. Or, more importantly, what she'd not done.

Looking back, Ivy knew that she hadn't accomplished half of the things she'd wanted to have done by now. All she'd managed to do was get married, and whilst that was great and her husband was a lovely, sexy doctor with a bum she could squeeze all day, it wasn't a life goal she'd worked for and achieved. It was just a thing that had happened to her. You can't be proud of things that happen to you, only things you work to make happen.

She was pretty sure that if she went back in time and told teenage Ivy that getting married was the only thing of note that she would have to her name, she'd have had books by Maya Angelou, Andrea Dworkin and Margaret Atwood thrown at her, and been scowled at through heavy black eyeliner.

"I think what I'm about to say is going to come as good news," said Hugh, leaning forwards on his elbows and smiling at her, cutting through her thoughts.

"It is?" asked Ivy. A promotion? Maybe that was better than a gift. It wasn't in a career she loved but still... if it was better than her current circumstances, she'd grab it with both hands.

"Definitely," said Hugh with a knowing look. "I think you and your husband will be quite thrilled to know... you're being made redundant!"

Ivy blinked. Her chest went cold. Her hands felt hot. "Wh... what?"

"Marvellous, eh?" said Hugh with what Ivy felt was unnervingly close to jazz hands.

Ivy pushed the bile back down into her stomach. "Why exactly will we be thrilled, sorry?"

"Well," said Hugh. "You've been married for a while now; I should think a nice little redundancy package and no pressure to get back to the office will suit you down to the ground!"

"Again..." said Ivy. "Why?"

Hugh adjusted his position awkwardly. "For when... you finally... you know..."

Ivy looked at him blankly.

"Start a family!" he said, the jazz hands creeping back in.

Okay, Mya was right. He needed a solid penis-punching.

"Start a..." she could barely get the words out. This wasn't supposed to happen. Especially not today. Not on her birthday. "It's my birthday..."

"I know!" said Hugh, definitely not reading the room. "Happy birthday!"

"And I've lost my job..."

"But gained your freedom!" enthused Hugh.

Ivy stared at him. He started to realise that this wasn't the wonderful news he'd apparently thought it was. His face fell and he started shifting uncomfortably in his seat. He looked at her hopefully, probably waiting for signs that she was coming round to his way of thinking, hoping to feel a little bit better about himself.

Ivy said nothing. She couldn't process her own thoughts, let alone comfort Hugh.

"Come on, Ivy.... You never wanted to be here anyway," he said, trying to placate her. "Let's be honest. You're obviously not happy here. We can all tell. Now you can go and find what you want in the world!"

What she wanted in the world? A steady income, a reliable job, pleasant enough work colleagues, opportunities for promotion... of course that was what she wanted. Why wouldn't it be? She stared at him, her mouth hanging open, words sticking in her throat before they could take form in her mouth. Probably for the best, to be fair. Every word forming in her mind was a swear word. The kind that made her mother scold her, even now.

Her eyes started to burn. *Shit. Don't cry, don't cry!*

The lingering silence seemed to be making Hugh uncomfortable. He cleared his throat several times and made some gestures that were supposed to indicate something that Ivy couldn't decipher because she was too busy trying to stop herself from falling apart and losing whatever shred of dignity she had left.

"It's effective immediately," said Hugh. Apparently, Ivy's silent internal screaming was finally too much for him. "If you could just pop over to Tom in HR, he's got some paperwork to process with you then you can run along and start your birthday celebrations early!"

She wasn't going to cry. She was going to be dignified and calm and completely in control at all times. She held tears back, got up, and headed for the door. Before she opened it, she hesitated then turned back to Hugh, who looked a bit nervous. "Why me?"

Hugh smiled at her awkwardly. "Just lucky I guess."

Ivy left before he could wave any more jazz hands at her.

***

Ivy filled a cardboard box with her things: a photo of her and Steven on their wedding day, a notepad she had filled with doodles and ideas, and a sad little cactus she'd bought because she killed all other plants. She left the cakes and the chocolates. Helen watched her.

"You okay?" she asked.

Ivy shrugged. Was she okay? She was thirty. She was unemployed. And she had to confess to her very successful and proud husband that she was thirty and unemployed. Of course she wasn't bloody okay. What a stupid fucking question.

"Yeah," she said. "I'm okay."

"Good," said Helen. "You never wanted to be here anyway."

Why did everybody keep saying that?! Like anybody had a clue what Ivy wanted!

Ivy grimaced a smile at her, then headed out of the office, keeping her head down. A couple of people poked their heads out of their cubicles to catch her eye and say goodbye, but Ivy just nodded in their direction and escaped. She couldn't face it. Not today.

Outside she took a breath of fresh air and went to the bench where she often ate her lunch in the summer. There was bird shit on it. She didn't care.

She sat down and put her head between her knees. Just deep, soothing breaths. In through the nose, out through the mouth. It would be fine. Of course it would be fine. She'd had jobs before, she could get jobs again. She'd done some shit jobs, mind...

No, it was fine. It had to be fine. Should she call Steven? No... definitely not. He'd start telling her all the things she should do immediately and she needed some time to scream into the void before she could process advice about what steps to take next.

She took a deep breath. She could call her mother?

Okay, she was clearly losing her mind.

Thirty and unemployed.

Fuck.

There was only one thing she wanted to do. And only two people she could possibly do it with.

She took her phone out of her bag and made a call. Three minutes later she headed for Verso.

***

"Dude," said Mya as Ivy approached the table where her best friends, Mya Shaw and Julia Jones, were waiting for her with an open bottle of wine and three large glasses.

"I know," said Ivy, sitting down heavily.

"That boss of yours is an absolute cun..."

"Mya!" snapped Julia.

"Fine," grumbled Mya and folded her arms as Julia filled a wine glass and pushed it over to Ivy.

"What am I going to tell Steven?" Ivy wailed, then dropped her face flat on the table.

"Steven will be fine!" Julia insisted, rubbing her back gently. "He's got a good job now!"

Ivy moaned miserably into the wooden tabletop. His income wasn't the issue. They'd worked hard to get him to the position he was in and they both benefited from his financial success. The issue was his opinion of Ivy. And it was Ivy's opinion of Ivy, which right now was low and crumbling lower.

She'd never been unemployed; even when she'd been at university, she'd worked in the student bar. That was where she'd met Mya, who liked to hide out in the basement smoking weed when she was supposed to be bringing up new barrels.

"I hate my life," Ivy wailed.

She only ever got to indulge her melodramatic tendencies around her friends, Steven found that behaviour irritating and her mother went into full mother hen mode, so there was no way she wasn't going to indulge right now.

"I know, I know," soothed Julia. "It's shit. But it'll be okay. I promise."

"And it's not like you can't get another one," said Mya. "The cun... erm... douchebag will write you a good reference, won't he?"

"So I can move from one shitty sales job to another shitty sales job," she said glumly, sitting up. "And watch my life drift away in yet another cubicle in yet another office. Day in. Day out. No dreams beyond what I'm having for lunch. Until the day I die."

"Have a drink," said Mya, pushing Ivy's wine towards her before refilling her own glass and smiling at the waitress, giving the empty bottle a little wiggle.

Ivy obediently picked up her glass and downed it. She set the glass down heavily and screwed up her face. Perhaps now she was thirty she shouldn't do things like getting drunk in the afternoon with her friends. But fuck it, now wasn't the time to be worrying about it.

"It's my birthday," she wailed. "This is the worst thing that could possibly happen on my birthday!"

"It'll get better," said Julia. "We'll get you through this tiny blip."

"Tiny blip, my arse," grumbled Ivy.

"And it's definitely not the worst thing to happen on your birthday," said Mya.

"It's not?" asked Ivy.

"Remember your nineteenth when you snogged Brendan Walker then puked on his shoes?"

"Oh yeah," said Ivy.

"Oh! And remember your twenty-first when you got chucked out of that club because you were attempting to perform a strip tease on the podium but couldn't get your shoe off and fell over?"

"You're such a knob," Ivy said, laughing.

"I think we have, in fact, proven that it is you who is the knob," said Mya with a knowing look.

The juxtaposition of wild and creative Mya with sensible and wise Julia was a combination that, on paper, should never work. But it did. And it always had. Aside from the true love the two women had for one another, Ivy felt that when they were together, both sides of her personality had found their soulmates.

The waitress brought over another bottle of wine and set it on the table.

"Enjoy," she said. Ivy noted that the waitress had a slightly judgemental tone that she did not care for. But fuck it, she hadn't lost her job.

Ivy picked up the bottle and refilled her glass. She should probably eat something. Something with fat and bread.

"You know what the worst thing is?" she asked them, immediately forgetting that she should be eating, and swilling the wine on the table as she gesticulated.

"What?" asked Mya.

"I hated that job," she said. "Hated it. I made big with how much I appreciated the whole steady income and stuff because that's what I had to do for Steven. But it was a crap job and I loathed every minute of it."

"I'm not surprised," said Mya. "It was the least Ivy job ever."

Julia nodded in agreement and sipped her wine.

"But I'm actually devastated that I lost it!" wailed Ivy. "Why did this happen to me? I mean seriously. This wasn't supposed to be my life! I had dreams and hopes and plans and now... now I'm gutted that I've lost this stupid job that I didn't even want in the first place!"

"Oh love," said Julia, her dark eyes dropping.

"I'm serious," said Ivy, leaning in towards them. "I think I was actually planning on living out my working days in a beige office with a grey carpet doing a boring job... all because it just wasn't *too* bad. If you'd told me on my twentieth birthday that on my thirtieth birthday, instead of being an architect, I'd be... this..." Ivy sighed and put her head in her hands. "I swear I'd have drowned myself in those godawful tequila shots you made me do, Mya."

Julia rubbed her arm, her perfectly manicured nails shining beautifully. Julia always looked so perfect. Even Mya somehow managed to make her pink hair and piercings style look effortlessly trendy. Ivy, in her grey pencil skirt and beige cardigan, looked every bit the miserable failure she was.

She rubbed a snotty tear on her sleeve and looked at her friends sadly.

"Please, tell me, how did this happen to me?"

Ivy picked up her wine and took a deep drink, before noticing Julia and Mya were exchanging a look over the top of their pinot. She knew what they were thinking, but she really didn't want to explore it right now.

Ivy picked up her wine again. Wine helped.

Julia rearranged her features into a broad and enthusiastic smile. "I think it's time for her present, don't you, Mya?"

Mya was less committed to the performance, probably wanting to delve into the root causes of Ivy's failed career prospects, but acquiesced and pulled an envelope out of her bag. An envelope gift! Envelope gifts could be excellent.

"What is it?" she asked them, taking the envelope and opening it. She pulled out an appointment card for that afternoon at the very high end and pricey salon, Carmelle's, where Julia always went. Ivy had never even set foot inside. Mya hadn't either, but that was less because of price, and more because Mya favoured the funky places where her pink hair could be chopped, bleached, shaved or spiked, according to whatever whim she was feeling in the moment, whilst she listened to metal music.

"The works," said Julia squeezing her arm. "All arranged and paid for. You're going to feel fabulous after that!"

"And look so good that Steven might not even bother with your swanky dinner and take you straight home to bed," said Mya with a wink.

Ivy laughed. "I want the dinner."

"Well, after food you can get a good ravishing," said Mya. "You're going to look bloody gorgeous."

Julia held up a glass. "To Ivy; thirty, unemployed, but bloody gorgeous."

"Bloody gorgeous!" repeated Mya as Ivy laughed. They clinked glasses and drank.

"Thanks guys," said Ivy. "This is so lush."

Julia leaned over and kissed her cheek, before finishing the last of her wine. "Right," she said, standing up and picking up her leather briefcase. "I've got to get back to the office, but Mya can stay, so I'll see you tomorrow, okay?"

"See you tomorrow," said Ivy.

Julia gave them a wave and headed out, her high heels click-clacking as she went. When she was out of the restaurant, Mya grabbed Ivy's hand excitedly with a mischievous look on her freckled face. "You've got two hours 'til your appointment..." she said.

"So...?" asked Ivy.

"Tequila!"

Chapter Two

Two hours later, Ivy was weaving her way towards Carmelle's carrying her box of things from work and feeling significantly more chipper.

She'd had more tequila than was sensible, followed by a massive pizza with a side of curly fries, then a chocolate brownie with ice cream. Her absolute chronic misery had been suppressed and she was excited for her pampering session. Hopefully, by the end of it she would look so good that Steven would be immediately forgiving and understanding about the slight change in employment circumstances.

She pushed open the door of Carmelle's and stepped inside. The air felt clean, with a slight fragrance that she imagined was similar to what Princess Kate probably smelled like. Everything was bronze and shimmery, and the floor tiles were so very shiny that she clamped her thighs together, convinced they were acting as a mirror to her M&S knickers.

Glancing around the corner to where rows of mirrors and chairs were lined up next to beautiful vases of flowers, Ivy observed the glamorous clientele. Every single one of them looked like a bloody model. She felt decidedly frumpy and every bit her thirty years of age.

Ivy hiccupped and held her head high, fixing an almost perfectly sober and confident smile on her face as she approached the reception desk, where a young woman was tapping away on a computer.

"Hello there!" said Ivy. Loudly. *Fuck's sake, get a grip Ivy.*

The young woman looked up at her and raised an eyebrow. "Welcome to Carmelle's, do you have an appointment?"

"I do have an appointment!" Ivy insisted, apparently not getting a grip and allowing the tequila to be her volume control. "I've got an appointment... on this card... here." Ivy handed over the card, her insides howling at her own awkwardness.

The young woman took the card and inspected it as if it could be a forgery and she was an expert in telling salon appointment card fakes from genuine ones.

"Ivy, is it?" she asked, setting the card down and tapping on the computer.

"That's right," said Ivy. "Ivy Rhodes."

"My name's China, and I'll be looking after you today," she said, eying Ivy up and down as she stood up.

"Oh well, thank you very much, China!" said Ivy, adjusting her hold on the box.

"That looks heavy," said China. "D'you want a hand?"

"No, I've got it, don't worry!" said Ivy enthusiastically, desperately wishing she could agree to the help without somehow proving herself to be both too hapless and too drunk to be in there.

"Okay, well if you'd like to come this way, Ms Rhodes," said China, leading her past the reception desk, past several of the models who were being tinted and coiffed, and to a chair in the middle of the room.

Ivy forced herself to be cool about the fact that the mirror was surrounded by lightbulbs, like the kind of mirror seven-year-old Ivy had begged her mother to get her, as China pulled the seat out for her to sit down in.

"Your booking says we're giving you the complete package," said China, examining Ivy's head, lifting up sections of her long brown hair and peering at them suspiciously, as though checking for lice. "Something special?"

"It's my birthday," said Ivy. "I'm going out for dinner with my husband."

"Well happy birthday," said China. "Can I get you a glass of prosecco to celebrate?"

"Yes please!" enthused Ivy.

"No problem, sweetie," said China, patting her on the shoulder. "I'll be right back. Why don't you check out some magazines and see if you can find a new look you'd like me to give you."

Ivy watched China sashay away through the salon then turned back to admire the mirror. Prosecco and a lightbulb mirror were the highlight of her day, which was actually just a little bit pathetic, but still. A highlight was a highlight.

Looking around, she completely understood why Julia loved this place. Julia was the most elegant and classy woman Ivy had ever known, even back in their early 20's when Ivy was still vomming up Blue WKD. And, quite predictably, as Ivy had gone on to a middling career in a middling company doing a middling job, Julia had shot up the ranks at her advertising firm and was well respected and admired in her industry.

Ivy picked up the magazine on the top of the stack in front of the mirror. She started to flick through the pages when she heard her phone vibrating. She put the magazine on top of the stack and rooted into her handbag. It was

Steven. She felt her stomach drop. Maybe it was best to tell him now. Get it over with. By the time they were out for dinner he'd have had time to process it. Yes, that would be better. Maybe they'd be able to enjoy the evening without focusing on it.

"Hi Steven," she said into the phone, trying to sound happy. "I'm so glad you called. I really need to talk to you."

"Ivy," said Steven, his voice oddly far away. "I need to talk to you too."

"What about?" she asked. Had something happened at work? He sounded didn't sound right. "What's happened? I'm in this fancy salon, Mya and Julia arranged it for me, but I'll be home soon. I've had the worst day and..."

"Ivy..." Steven interrupted again. Something was wrong. He sounded wrong.

"Has something come up?" Ivy asked tentatively. Of course, something had come up. Why wouldn't she lose her job and have her birthday night out with her husband cancelled on the same day? Typical. "Has something happened? Are you going to be late? Are you..."

"Ivy," Steven said again, his voice sharper this time. She startled a little. He sounded angry with her.

"Here you go," said China, reappearing at Ivy's side and making her jump. She put a glass of prosecco down in front of the mirror and started examining Ivy's head again.

"Thanks!" said Ivy to China, before going back to Steven. "I've just been given prosecco, so I guess at least one thing is improving today, I mean..."

"Ivy, just stop talking," said Steven sharply. "You need to listen."

Ivy's palms got sweaty. Had he lost his job too? No... no fate couldn't be that cruel. But it was definitely something serious. She picked up the prosecco and took an anxious swig.

Behind her, China seemed to sense that Ivy needed a bit of space and backed away from her respectfully, pretending to examine a magazine whilst surreptitiously listening in.

"Ivy," said Steven again. The way he kept saying her name, like it was unfamiliar in his mouth, like it tasted strange, was making her feel sick. "This isn't easy for me to say."

"What isn't?" Ivy asked, her voice straining.

"I've moved out."

"Moved out... of what?"

"Our house."

"Our... house?" Ivy squeaked, her tongue was fluffy, her eyes were swollen, her stomach was full of rocks and soup. What the hell was going on?

"I'm sorry, Ivy," he said. "This hasn't been working for a long time, and I just can't do it anymore."

"It's... my birthday..." Ivy stuttered.

"I know. It's shit timing..."

"You think?" Ivy cried, louder than she had intended, so around the room eyes turned to stare at her.

"Yeah," said Steven gruffly. "So, erm... I'll see you around, yeah?"

The phone went dead. Ivy stared at her reflection in the mirror. She felt numb. She slowly took the phone away from her ear and hung up.

Did that just happen? Did her husband just end their marriage over the phone... in public... on her birthday? What... the hell...

Behind her, China approached her again, a cautious look on her face. "Are you okay?"

Ivy looked at her in the reflection of the mirror. China's face was full of concern and curiosity. Ivy nodded slowly.

"Ready to get going?" China asked, lifting up a piece of Ivy's hair.

Ivy's eyes dropped from China's and she met her own in the reflection. *What just happened?*

She nodded again. She didn't know what else to do. She couldn't think. She couldn't speak. She was sitting in front of a lightbulb-encrusted mirror, gripping a glass of prosecco so tightly she feared she might snap the stem, but she couldn't loosen her grip. She couldn't move her arm to set the glass down. Her body was frozen on the outside and a swirling vortex of pain on the inside.

"Is the prosecco okay?" asked China.

Ivy looked up at China again. She lifted the glass to her mouth and downed the contents. Because... why not? She forced her arm forwards and pushed the glass with an unpleasant screech onto the shelf under the mirror.

"Are you okay, honey?" asked China, again, putting her hands on Ivy's shoulders.

Ivy swallowed every feeling down. She wouldn't lose her shit there. Not right there. Not in the swanky salon in front of all those people. All she had to do was get through the appointment and get home. Then she could scream and cry and rage all she wanted. But right now, all she wanted to do was get through it. Just get through it.

"Yes," she said, forcing a smile onto her face, cursing her eyeballs for stinging with tears she would not let out. "I'm fine."

"Okay," said China, nodding. "Let's get to work. You've got some real potential under here."

Ivy allowed her to drape a shiny black cloak across her shoulders. She had her hair washed; she listened to China talk about Love Island; she smiled as much as she could bear to whilst her hair was primped and teased into a chignon on the back of her head. She forced her hand to stop shaking whilst her nails were done. She refused to allow her eyes to cry off the mascara that was applied to them.

She sat still and she didn't scream.

Finally, China finally spun the chair around so Ivy could admire herself in the dream mirror.

"Look at you," said China, clasping her hands together proudly. "You look amazing!"

"Thank you," said Ivy, peering at herself. Her face was painted, her hair was perfect. Her eyes were hollow and haunted, dark holes of despair dying quietly beneath the glitz and glamour that surrounded them.

"Do you like it?" China asked hopefully.

Ivy forced her most convincing smile onto her face. Her hair was beautiful, her nails were spangly, her make-up was elegant. Ivy had to admit that China had done a superb job. And she hated everything about it. She wanted to punch the mirror, smash the image of a glamorous woman headed out to have a romantic dinner and champagne with her loving husband. It was an illusion. It was fake. It had been an illusion for a long time, according to Steven.

"I love it," said Ivy. "Thank you."

Ivy picked up her box of belongings and walked through the salon, her legs forcing their way through a swamp of resistance, making every step harder and harder, every movement painful. She was heavy and flat and dizzy.

Maybe she'd drink the bottle of champagne she'd bought herself to have with Steven before dinner. Maybe she'd smash it in the sink and eat a whole cheesecake. Maybe she'd use a piece of the broken glass to cut her wrists.

She instinctively shuddered at that last one. Not that.
That was too far.

But getting rat-arsed and passing out in a pool of vomit
felt like an appropriate response to everything that the day
had thrown at her.

Ivy climbed the steps to their front door. Before she put
her key in, she hesitated. Walking into an empty house
with all this hair and make-up felt so pitiful and pathetic
that she needed a moment to wallow in just how ghastly
her life was. She determined that before she got drunk and
passed out, she'd take a shower and wash off the mockery
of this glamorous look.

She took a deep breath, put they key in the lock, and
stepped into the dark living room, ready to accept her fate.

"SURPRISE!"

Chapter Three

Ivy pressed herself back against the door as the box of things fell from her hands with a crash onto the floor.

Holy. Fucking. Shit.

The living room lights came on, party poppers flung confetti at her, and around the room Ivy saw the smiling and excited faces of everybody she cared about. Well. Almost everybody.

Feeling bile rising in her throat, Ivy forced herself to plaster on yet another fake smile.

"Wow!" she forced out, her hands trembling as she tucked her hair behind her ear and forced her knees rigid to stop her legs from buckling.

"Ivy!" cried her mother, hurrying towards her with a glass of champagne and embracing her tightly.

"Hi Mum!" said Ivy, allowing kisses to land on her cheeks before accepting the glass that was forced into her hand. She spotted Mya and Julia over her mother's shoulder. They gave her theatrical winks and thumbs ups before grabbing drinks.

"Happy birthday, baby!" cried her mother stepping back and holding out Ivy's hands, looking her up and down. "You look absolutely glorious!"

"Well... thanks!" said Ivy, trying not to let the absolute agonising despair that was swilling around her guts to display itself on her face.

Her mother looked at her curiously. Shit. She tried to make her smile as natural and calm as possible. She didn't need her mother's Spidey-sense for Ivy's moods to be alerted at that very moment.

"Are you alright, darling?" her mother asked, her eyes filling with concern.

"Ivy!" said her father, ambling towards her and thankfully distracting her mother.

"Dad," Ivy greeted him with a hug, and he clinked his champagne glass against her own. She smiled at him as politely as she could, then downed her glass in one go, figuring the idea of a sober birthday ended about six hours earlier, so why stop now? "How are you?"

"Well," said her father, looking around and looking as uncomfortable as Ivy felt. "At least there's booze."

Ivy nodded, eyeing her empty glass and wondering if she could sneak off and find more. She looked around to see if there was a bottle close by and spotted Mya and Julia chatting with Julia's husband Fred, in the corner. Mya turned and gesticulated at her to join them. Ivy went to move in their direction, but her father put his arm around her.

"Where's young Steven then?" he asked.

Ivy froze. She hadn't come up with a cover story because she hadn't known she'd need a cover story and now she couldn't think of a cover story. "I... He... Uh..." Ivy floundered.

"Ivy?" said her mum. "Where is he?"

"He had to stay late at the hospital," she said through gritted teeth. She couldn't fall apart now. She had to hold it together. She had to. Glancing up she saw that Mya and Julia had become aware of the tension radiating from her. They were watching her closely, occasionally whispering a comment to one another.

"Oh no!" said her mother, rubbing Ivy on the arm. "Oh love. How disappointing."

"Yep!" said Ivy, her icy smile starting to hurt.

"No wonder you're tense," she said, giving Ivy's hand a squeeze. "What a shame!"

"Yep," said Ivy. "Yep, it is. Certainly. A shame. It is a damn shame."

"At least you know he's doing something good, though, baby," said her mum, rubbing her arm and looking so well-intentioned that Ivy wanted to scream in her face. "His job is so important."

Ivy's jaw was starting to lock. She had to stop smiling. She stared at Mya and Julia.

"You know what I always say?" asked her father.

"What, Dad?" asked Ivy, wondering which of the many things it was that he was referring to that he always said despite never actually having said it.

"Never trust a man with a built-in excuse," said her dad, chuckling. "Too easy to exploit. That kind of power goes to a man's head!"

"Mrs Reynolds!" said Julia, appearing suddenly at Ivy's mother's elbow.

"Mr Reynolds!" said Mya, appearing by Ivy's father.

"Your hair," said Ivy's dad, peering at Mya. "It's pink!"

"Well observed, Mr Reynolds," said Mya, pointing at him. "You never miss a trick."

"Mya! Julia!" said Ivy's mother, smiling warmly. "Lovely to see you girls. How are you both?"

"We're fine thanks," said Julia, linking her arm through Ivy's.

"And how are Sebastian and Fred?" asked Ivy's mother.

"Fred's just over there," said Julia, gesturing towards her husband who was chatting to somebody incredibly boring-looking that Ivy didn't know and assumed was married to one of her equally dull cousins. "And Sebastian went the way of Jeremy, Lorenzo, Annabelle, Sarah and Matt!"

"Damn right, he did," said Mya, raising her glass.

"Well good riddance," said Ivy's mum. "He was a pretentious twat."

Mya nodded in agreement. "That he was."

Ivy stared into her own empty glass. What the hell was she supposed to do? This was a nightmare. She had to get out of there.

"You're empty," observed Julia, pointedly. "Excuse us, Mr and Mrs Reynolds. We're going to steal the birthday girl away for a bit."

Julia steered Ivy towards the kitchen, Mya trotting along behind them.

"Happy birthday Ivy!" called Hayley, one of the dull cousins, as she passed.

Ivy forced a wan smile onto her face, but Julia moved her on fast before Hayley could stop them and interrupt their mission.

They slipped into the kitchen and Mya pushed the door closed behind herself as Ivy leaned against the counter, her head back and her eyes closed. She took several deep breaths. In through the nose and out through the mouth. In through the nose. Out through the mouth. Don't panic. Don't freak out. Just get through it.

Julia put a hand on Ivy's arm as Mya refilled their champagne glasses. "Hey," she said gently. Ivy looked at her. "Are you alright?"

Ivy shook her head, keeping her eyes closed. "No."

"Want to talk about it?"

Not now. She couldn't now. Too many people. Too much going on. Not now.

She took another deep breath and looked at her friends' worried faces. "I'm just... overwhelmed."

"Sorry," said Mya, handing her the glass of champagne. "I know it's shit timing with the whole redundancy stuff to deal with. Steven cooked this stupid party up and now the bastards not even here!"

"St... Steven? Did this?" Ivy asked, her head spinning. Steven knew? He knew she was heading into a surprise party and he still did this to her?

"Your mother took care of most of the guest list," said Julia. "Hence some of the less desirable cousins being in attendance, but yeah, it was Steven's idea."

"I think he was trying to be romantic," said Mya. "He meant well."

Ivy slid onto the floor and sat heavily on the lino. She drank the contents of her champagne glass and held the glass up to Mya.

"Maybe some water?" advised Julia, getting a glass down from the cupboard.

"Wine," said Ivy burping fruitily. "Just the wine."

Mya glanced at Julia. They had a little conversation with their eyes.

"GUYS!" wailed Ivy. "I'm right HERE! Stop parenting me!"

Julia sighed as Mya refilled the wine glass and handed it back down. Ivy took it and watched grumpily as Julia filled the glass with water anyway, before setting it down on the counter above Ivy's head.

Ivy's head was swimming. Julia was right. She was trashed. She just didn't have the strength to do anything except *be* trashed at this point. At least it provided a vague sense of numbness.

"Alright, gimme the water," she mumbled.

Julia handed her the glass then sat down on the floor by her side.

"How did he take it?" Mya asked, sitting cross-legged on the floor opposite her.

"Take what?" asked Ivy.

"The redundancy..." said Julia quietly, her face quizzical.

"Oh right. That." Ivy took a swig of the champagne. "I've not told him yet."

"Ah love," said Julia, crouching down next to her. "No wonder you're stressed with that weighing on you. He'll be home soon."

"HA!" Ivy scoffed, then took another drink.

"Oh babe," said Mya, rubbing her foot. "You're wankered."

"Yup," said Ivy, leaning back and closing her eyes again.

She wanted to tell them - just let it all out - but with a house full of people she had no choice but to grit her teeth and hold it together just a little bit longer. The last thing she needed was boring cousin Hayley and the woman she used to work with in the doctor's surgery hearing her have a meltdown over her failed marriage and her broken heart.

"Come on," said Mya. "Let's get that drunken ass out there to enjoy the party and you can put telling Steven out of your mind for a bit!"

Steven. She felt a stabbing pain in her chest. His name hurt. Physically hurt. Her stomach churned.

"I'm going to be sick," Ivy muttered.

"On your feet," said Julia, leaping up before helping Ivy to her feet and spinning her round to face the sink in a manoeuvre they'd perfected in Fresher's week.

Ivy gripped the sink tightly, bile rising in her throat. Julia rubbed her back gently as Mya held her hair back.

Her lunchtime pizza and ice cream, blended into a stinking, burning mess with tequila and prosecco, erupted out of her. Julia soothed her whilst Mya turned the tap on to sloosh the mess down the plughole. Ivy stared at it as it swilled away and felt another wave coming.

"Better out than in, babe," said Julia gently, as Ivy retched.

When it was all gone, Ivy stood up and looked at her friends hopelessly. "Is it obvious?" she asked.

Mya fetched some tissues, licked one, and gently dabbed at the corners of Ivy's eyes, picking up ruined eyeliner, whilst Julia got a wet cloth onto a vomit mark on her cardigan.

"You're beautiful," said Julia. "But your breath stinks."

"There's Tic Tacs in the cupboard," said Ivy, waving a hand vaguely.

Mya rooted around until she found them, then popped the cap open and tipped a few into Ivy's hand. "One won't cut it, love," she said.

Ivy crunched the mints up and took a sip of her water. "Okay," she said. "I'm ready."

Mya and Julia slipped an arm each into Ivy's, and carefully led her back into the living room. She smiled at everyone as best as she could and was shown a big pile of gifts. She resisted the pressure to open them, public performance of gratitude a step too far when so much performance was already required of her. She hugged and air-kissed everybody, even Hayley, and was forced to reminisce about memories of birthdays past. Birthdays where Steven had surprised her with other things. Birthdays when she had been happy.

"Remember the trip to Rome?" enthused Tina from high school, looking dreamy-eyed. "The Facebook pictures were amazing. He's so romantic."

Go fuck yourself, Tina.

"Oh, remember the one to Paris!" said Hayley. "Didn't you go on that one Mya?"

"Yep," said Mya, sounding decidedly less enamoured with the memory.

"Which boyfriend was that with?" asked Hayley, innocently.

Mya gave Hayley a look which made Hayley take a step backwards and fall down to sit on the sofa.

Ivy nodded along as they talked about her amazing experiences and her beautiful relationship. They were right, Steven had taken her to Rome and he'd taken her to Paris. He'd filled the living room with sunflowers, he'd booked every seat in a cinema so they could watch a movie alone, and now he'd arranged a surprise party with all her favourite people. Wasn't Steven the best? Wasn't he just the absolute, world-class, wonderfully, perfect best?

Screw this. Ivy drank more champagne.

Ivy could tell Julia and Mya knew something more was going on. They kept exchanging furtive looks and following her around, trying to keep her buoyed. If anyone engaged her in conversation for too long they interrupted and found reasons for her to leave. Every so often Julia pushed a glass of water or a piece of pizza into her hand and encouraged her to consume things that weren't alcohol.

Bless their kindness, they didn't push her to talk. Not then. Not with all those people.

After the final cousin had left, and Julia and Mya were busily gathering abandoned plates and bottles, her mother gave Ivy a last hug.

"Lunch tomorrow?" she asked her, tucking a strand of Ivy's hair behind her ear before gently resting a hand on her cheek. Ivy put her own hand up on top of her mother's and nodded, feeling her mother's soft, warm hand against her face.

She'd run out of words. If she spoke again it would all come out. Not now. Not when she was drunk and her father was swaying merrily at the door, humming Umbrella by Rihanna.

"Verso?" suggested her mother, her voice full of worry. "Twelve thirty? My treat?"

Ivy nodded again and gave her mother a kiss on the cheek. Ivy could tell she wanted to ask questions, pinpoint the source of Ivy's discomfort and then kill it. But she didn't.

"Emmeline!" her dad called from the door, peering towards them with a drunken squint.

Ivy's mum rolled her eyes with a smile. "Coming, dear," she said fondly before turning back to Ivy. "I love you, poppet."

Ivy's eyes burned but she smiled again. She couldn't speak. She wanted to. She wanted to sob to her mother about all the pain she was in and the betrayal that was making her want to throw up again. But she couldn't. Not now.

Julia watched the exchange then stepped forward, business-like and efficient. "Have a safe journey," she said, an arm around Ivy's mum's shoulders. "Do you need help getting him into the taxi?" she asked, as Ivy's father started to twirl on the spot, apparently lost in the second movement of whatever song the tune he was now humming was supposed to represent.

Ivy's mother opened the door and her father ambled through it. "Em!" he shouted. "The moon's out!"

"Yes love," she said, rolling her eyes at Julia.

"It's majestic!"

Ivy's mum patted Julia on the arm. "I've been getting that man into cabs after parties for nearly forty years," she said with a laugh. "I'm a pro now."

Julia laughed politely, gave them a little wave, then closed the door on Ivy's parents and turned around sharply. "What's going on?"

Ivy felt a gut-wrenching sob burst from her gut, then an animalistic howl wail from her chest as her knees buckled. She fell down, her hands on the carpet in front of her, as she sobbed. Finally, brutally, sobbed.

Mya and Julia raced to her, falling onto their knees at her side and putting their arms around her. Ivy fell against Julia, as Julia held her and Mya stroked her, kissed her cheeks, and held her hand. For several minutes they sat with her silently, letting her cry, just tenderly being with her in her despair.

When her wailing had slipped into a quiet weeping, Julia stroked her hair from her face. "What happened?" she asked.

"It's... St..." Ivy tried. She couldn't. "Steven..." She couldn't say it.

Julia tensed beneath her. She felt Mya's hands stiffen on her back.

"What did he do?" demanded Julia, her voice suddenly dark.

Ivy finally forced the words out. "He's gone."

"Gone where?" asked Mya, her fingertips digging into Ivy's arm.

Ivy sat up and wiped her eyes on her sleeve. She looked at them, embarrassed and ashamed, drunk and broken. "I don't know," she whispered, wiping her eyes again and smearing mascara and eyeliner across her hands and clothes. "He didn't say. He just said... it's over."

"When did this happen?" asked Julia.

"He... he phoned me... today... at Carmelle's..."

Julia stood up, letting Ivy slide into a heap on the floor. "HE DID FUCKING WHAT?"

Chapter Four

Mya stood up. "Say that again…" she said.

Ivy looked up at her two friends. Their fury was oddly comforting. She was right to be angry. She was right to be upset. She hadn't really doubted it, but seeing her friends' reactiona had just confirmed it. Her emotions were justified. She is allowed to feel like this.

She took a deep breath.

"Phoned me," said Ivy. "At Carmelle's… I was on the chair surrounded by all those glamorous model-type women who go there, looking at a hair magazine… but that's not important. The girl who was doing my hair was getting me a prosecco and I was sitting in the chair in front of the mirror with all the lightbulbs round it, and I was feeling like Liza Minelli, and…"

"I'm getting the vodka," said Mya, standing up and storming out.

Ivy stopped talking. She felt the tears coming back. It may be righteous pain, but it was still pain.

Julia sat back down, landing heavily on the carpet next to Ivy.

"So, you're telling me," she said, staring hard at Ivy's shoe. "That he ended your marriage… by phone."

"Yes," whispered Ivy, choking on her tears.

"On your birthday."

"Yes," sobbed Ivy, again.

"In public."

"Yes." Ivy was now about ready to drown herself in a vat of that tequila.

"And headed to your own surprise party," Mya added as she reappeared clutching a vodka bottle and three shot glasses that Ivy suspected hadn't been cleaned.

"That he planned!" Julia cried, throwing her arms into the air in exasperation.

"Drink," said Mya, pushing a shot glass at Ivy.

"I don't think I can," Ivy whispered.

"Shut up and drink your medicine," said Julia, taking a shot glass.

Ivy sighed and shot the vodka back. She winced and groaned as Mya refilled her glass. She was pretty sure this was how she was going to die. Here lies Ivy: Her husband abandoned her; her career was destroyed; and her blood alcohol levels were unfathomable.

"Oh God," she wailed, leaning back on the sofa.

"Am I allowed to say cunt now?" Mya asked Julia.

"Oh yeah," said Julia, squinting at her and screwing up her nose, the vodka having an effect. "Definitely."

"Cunt," said Mya. Julia winced. "Now drink."

Ivy and Julia drank as Mya refilled her own.

"He'll come back," said Julia, leaning back against the sofa, then letting out an impressive belch.

"You think?" asked Ivy, peering at the lamp. Lamp. Lamp was such a strange word. She hiccupped.

"He loves you!" cried Julia, sitting up and waving her arms around emphatically, knocking over the lamp that Ivy had been watching suspiciously. "You don't leave a five-year marriage for no reason!"

"Unless you're a cunt," said Mya, nodding sagely.

"Okay," said Julia, holding up a hand to Mya. "Now you absolutely must stop."

Mya shrugged and refilled the glasses. "Fine, I'll stop," she said, wobbling as she spoke. "As long as for now we drink. We can worry about Steven tomorrow."

Ivy nodded in agreement, though she wasn't certain what it was she was agreeing to. It could have been a tattoo on her right nipple for all she knew at this point.

"That's my girl!" said Mya. She clinked glasses with Ivy then they both drank.

Julia slid onto the floor.

***

There was a noise. A familiar noise. A ghastly noise.

Ivy put a hand to her head and groaned. What was making that noise of evil? Ringing. Ringing sounds of pain. "Aaaaarrrrggghhhhh!" she wailed.

"Fred?"

She heard Julia's voice as the evil noise stopped. Ivy pulled a pillow on her face. Her head hurt.

"Yeah, I stayed," said Julia, her voice sounding gruff and scratchy. "What?"

Ivy's gut's squirmed and surged. Was she dying? Her brain bumped against her skull and her eyeballs threatened to fall out of her face.

"Because Steven fucked off, that's why!"

Steven. Oh God. It all came back. Steven.

"No, of course she isn't!" Julia snapped.

Steven. He'd left her. Ivy felt sick rising in her guts. She needed to throw up.

"She doesn't know why."

She pulled the pillow off her face and tried to focus on the world beyond the pillow, but the light stabbed her. She pressed the pillow back into her face. Never again.

"Because she doesn't know, alright?!" Julia stomped past Ivy's head and started pacing up and down behind the sofa. How was she moving? Ivy couldn't move. Ivy was broken. "Well, he ended it over the phone like a fucking coward, so he's not your bloody mate anymore, Frederick!"

Ivy groaned and tried to sit up. She feared if she remained horizontal, she'd throw up in her mouth and drown. Scrambling at the back of the sofa, she managed to pull herself upright, her head swimming as she tried to hold it still. Julia gave her shoulder an affectionate squeeze as she stomped past again.

She peered across the room and saw Mya face down on the rug. Was she alive? Oh God, what if she wasn't?

Mya farted. She was alive.

"I'll be home in a bit," said Julia behind her. "Well, I can't! I'm gonna help Ivy clean up after the party and stuff!"

Ivy looked around. The empty vodka bottle was on the floor. Mess from the party strewn across the floor. It looked remarkably like their student house had always looked on a Saturday morning.

Julia sat down heavily next to Ivy, giving her a look of exasperation.

"They're your bloody parents! Cook for them yourself!" Julia rubbed her head and scrunched up her eyes.

Ivy tried to stand and promptly regretted it. She flumped back into the sofa again with a groan of agony.

"Fine," Julia sighed, leaning back and throwing her hand in the air. "Then make a reservation!"

Ivy tried to stand again. She slowly forced her body upright up and wobbled a bit. Oh God. Maybe puking would actually help. Better out than in. She slowly turned on the spot, testing out her limbs. They hurt. Everything hurt.

"Wherever you want! Jesus, Fred, I'm a little busy here!"

Ivy staggered towards the kitchen but tripped over Mya's leg and fell heavily down onto the armchair. Mya groaned. Ivy closed her eyes. She tried to remember the results from the last time she had Googled hangover cures. Something with tomato juice? Did she have tomato juice? She seemed to remember boring cousin Hayley sipping nervously on a Bloody Mary.

"Good. Right," said Julia. "Fine. See you soon."

Mya rolled over then moaned in despair, her hands over her face. Ivy wondered how you get vomit out of a rug - maybe that was what the tomato juice was for?

"Love you too." Julia hung up the phone and closed her eyes. "How's your head?" she asked Ivy.

"I'm dying," said Ivy, curling herself into the foetal position on the armchair and wondering if she was literally going to die.

"Me too," said Julia.

Ivy closed her eyes and felt the absolute chronic agony consume her. Despite the misery of the hangover from Hell, it didn't take long for the pain in her heart to overwhelm it.

"How could he do this to me?" she said quietly.

"I really don't know, babe," said Julia sadly, reaching out a hand and stroking Ivy's foot. "Probably a mid-life crisis."

"He's thirty-two," said Ivy, looking at her.

"Okay, a one-third life crisis then," said Julia with a sigh. "Listen, you've been there for him for years, right? You gave up on all your hopes and dreams to support him whilst he trained and qualified; cheered him on as he got his life together."

"Well...yeah," said Ivy.

"And now he's qualified, he's working," said Julia. "It's all done. You were going to buy a new place, maybe try for a baby, right?"

"Yeah, we talked about it. We had to wait until his career was stable," said Ivy. "We didn't want to rush into it. We'd said maybe in the future..."

"I think now might be the future," said Julia. "So, he's running scared. He's realised he's got to wear his big boy pants and he's being a pathetic man-child and hiding from the responsibility."

"You suck at being hungover," Mya groaned from the floor. "Stop using big words."

"I miss him so much," Ivy choked out, tears creeping out again.

"I know, darling," said Julia. She stood up and came over to Ivy, kneeling on the floor next to her. "I know. I'm so sorry."

"I don't know what to do," said Ivy, turning to look at Julia's concerned face.

"Well, for now, let's get this shit-hole cleaned up," said Julia, sounding far too sensible and competent for the amount of blood in her alcohol system. "We have to swallow an elephant."

"What the actual fuck, Julia?" demanded Mya.

"It's what my mum always taught me. When things seem like it's just too much to cope with, you think about how you'd swallow and elephant," said Julia. "You couldn't do it all at once, it's too big. So, you'd have to break it down into little pieces and take one at a time."

"That's disgusting," said Ivy, with a laugh. And it was, but she was beginning to see why Julia had managed to accomplish so much. Her life was an elephant she was determinedly swallowing.

"Now," said Julia, slapping her thighs and standing up. "You can wallow in misery, but you shouldn't have to wallow in empty beer bottles and half-eaten sausage rolls."

Ivy sighed and forced herself to her feet.

"Come on, Mya," said Julia. "You'll feel better if you get up."

"FALSE!"

Julia prodded Mya in the bum with her foot.

"Fuck off," grunted Mya. Julia plucked the sofa cushion from Mya's head and Mya wailed in despair. "Oh my God! I hate you!"

"I know," said Julia, picking up a bin bag. "But Ivy needs us. So; get up."

Mya groaned and rolled over. Gripping the coffee table, she pulled herself up, and swayed dangerously on the spot. She squinted at Ivy, her pink hair sticking at funny angles, green eyeliner smeared across her face.

"I blame Steven for this," Mya growled.

"Me too," said Julia.

"Me too," said Ivy.

Ivy turned to look at the room. Eat an elephant. Eat an elephant. Her head swayed and her stomach growled.

"Coffee," Mya said, wobbling and putting a hand on the wall to steady herself. "Before cleaning, coffee."

"What time is it?" asked Ivy, trying to find her phone. "I said I'd meet my mum for lunch."

"It's half ten," said Julia, looking at her glitzy wristwatch.

"I'm meeting my mum at twelve thirty," said Ivy, thinking hard and suffering for the effort. "So, I need to leave by twelve fifteen."

"There's time," said Julia. "Let's get coffee then crack on."

"Are you going to tell her?" Mya asked Ivy as they made their way, very slowly and very carefully, to the kitchen."

"Yes," said Ivy. "She's going to lose her shit, but at least it's in a public place so - in theory - that'll put her off committing any crimes."

"I dunno," said Julia. "She's going to unleash full Momma Bear."

"I know," said Ivy. "But she's going to find out eventually."

"And if she kills him," said Mya, pawing through cupboards like a feral animal at a bin as she looked for coffee. "It wouldn't be the worst thing."

Julia batted her out of the way and sorted out the coffee while Ivy and Mya sank into kitchen chairs and watched her.

Chapter Five

Ivy's mum was sitting with a cup of coffee and browsing the menu when Ivy found her way to Verso at twelve forty-five.

After one serious vomit explosion in the kitchen sink, which had required an entire bottle of bleach to deodorise, she and her friends had managed to get the house looking vaguely respectable. Ivy had washed all the abandoned plates and cups; Julia had busily applied Zoflora to every possible surface, and Mya had made encouraging noises and held bin bags open for them. Then Ivy'd changed her clothes, applied a hell of a lot of deodorant, and Mya had patched up the fancy Carmelle's makeup, so she looked significantly less dishevelled.

As Ivy approached, Emmeline looked up and smiled broadly. "Ivy, darling," she said. She came around the table to Ivy and kissed her cheek, then held her tenderly on both arms, tilting her hair to the side in that way mums do when they know something's up. "You're looking lovely. A bit green around the gills though."

"Hi Mum," Ivy tried to smile but her face was so sick of lying. "Yeah, me and the girls kept the party going after you'd left."

"Well, you three always did know how to have fun," said Ivy's mum with a fond chuckle as she went back to her seat. "Let's order some wine."

Ivy lowered herself into the chair opposite her mother. "I think I had enough last night."

"Nonsense," said Emmeline, looking around then waving her hand enthusiastically towards the young woman behind the bar. "Whatever's going on needs alcohol. I can tell."

Ivy shrugged. She wasn't going to argue. Maybe hair of the dog *was* what she needed, or maybe it would put her into a coma so she could stop dealing with the whole mess anyway. Her mother caught the attention of one of the servers, who hurried over.

"What can I get you?" asked the bubbly waitress, smiling at them both.

"Two Proseccos," said Emmeline, then glanced at Ivy. "No, make it a bottle. I have a feeling we're in for the long haul here."

"No problem!" said the waitress.

"Right," said Ivy's mum, sitting upright and looking serious. "Talk to me. What's going on?"

"I lost my job yesterday," said Ivy. She might as well start at the beginning. At least this was the bit that didn't make her want to scream. "They made me redundant."

"Oh Ivy," said her mum, taking her hand and giving it a squeeze. "And on your birthday. No wonder you're upset, darling. But honestly, you were always so much better than that place! Perhaps it's a blessing in disguise?"

"There's more," said Ivy, her eyes dropping.

"Okay?"

"It's Steven..." she started.

Her mother's eyes flashed and her jaw tensed. Momma Bear. "What did Steven do?"

"Steven... left me..."

Her mother sat very still for a moment then sharply sat bolt upright, looking around. "Where is that bloody prosecco?"

At the bar, the waitress caught her looking and held up a bottle with a nod and a smile.

"She's coming, Mum, give her a minute," said Ivy.

"Is that why the cowardly bastard didn't show up to your party?" she asked, turning back to Ivy, a dangerous look in her eyes.

"Yes."

"He thinks ending your marriage on your thirtieth birthday is acceptable, does he?"

"It gets worse," said Ivy.

Emmeline leaned in, her voice dark and low. "How much worse?"

"He did it over the phone," said Ivy. "While I was at the salon."

Ivy's mother shot onto her feet, her seat tipping over backwards with a loud clatter, and took her earrings out. Full Momma Bear. "WHERE IS HE?"

"Sit down, Mum!" Ivy hissed. It seemed that the threat of witnesses wasn't enough to dampen her mother's bloodlust.

"Tell me where he is!" she said, leaning forwards.

"I don't know, alright?" said Ivy, looking around embarrassed. "Sit down, Mum! And put your earrings back in. What are you going to do, fight him? He's half your age and you've got a dodgy hip!"

Emmeline Reynolds had the look of a middle-aged woman who was completely capable of taking down a thirty-two-year-old surgeon with the force of her venomous stare alone, but she acquiesced and picked up her chair before sitting back down. Ivy noted that the earrings did not go back in, nor did the shoulders release their coiled spring-like tension. But at least she was sitting.

The bubbly waitress approached with the bottle of prosecco and two glasses on a little tray. "Here we go, ladies!" she said, setting them down. "Are we having a little celebration?"

"No, we are not," said Emmeline.

"Just one of those days is it?" asked the waitress, pouring the prosecco out with a giggle. "I always say, you don't ever need an excuse for a bit of bubbly!"

Ivy wondered if she did always say that. To be fair, she looked like the kind of woman who had a 'Live Laugh Love' picture on the wall and got tipsy on a single glass of gin, so maybe she really did always say it. She probably had it embroidered on a cushion.

Emmeline picked up her glass and took a swig. Ivy came from a line of women who could drink significantly more than a single glass of gin. Which, given the situation, was lucky really.

Apparently oblivious to the excruciating tension at the table, the waitress took a notepad out of her pocket. "Are we ready to order?"

"No," said Ivy's mother through gritted teeth. "We are not."

"A couple more minutes?" asked Ivy, apologetically. "Please?"

"Oh, sure," said the waitress. "Just give me a wave and I'll be right over."

"Please go away now," said Emmeline.

"Oh!" said the waitress. "Okay!"

She hurried away looking hurt and Ivy sighed.

"You didn't have to take it out on the waitress, Mum!" whispered Ivy. "SHE didn't leave me!"

Emmeline took a deep breath then another big swing of prosecco. "Okay," she said. "Tell me everything. What exactly did the weasel say to you?"

"He said it wasn't easy for him…"

"FOR HIM?" her mother shrieked. More heads turned in their direction and Ivy felt her cheeks burning.

"Mum!"

"What else did the little cockroach say?" Weasels, cockroaches, Ivy wondered what kind of critter Steven would be labelled next.

"He said that he's moved out because it wasn't working. And he knows that it's shit timing."

Ivy watched as her mother processed the information. It involved a lot of muttering under her breath but at least she wasn't shouting animal names anymore.

"Is there somebody else?" she asked eventually.

"I don't know."

"Where's he moved to?"

"I don't know."

"Is he going to keep paying the rent?"

"I don't know."

"Is he…"

"Let me stop you there, Mum," said Ivy, reaching saturation point on the quizzing. "I told you everything I know. He moved out while I was at work. His stuff's gone. I don't know why, and I don't know where."

Ivy's mother refilled her own prosecco then pushed Ivy's still-full glass towards her. Just as misery loves company, apparently so does stress drinking.

Emmeline took a long drink from her glass then set it down. She stared at her hands, her face hard.

"You gave up everything for that man," she said after a moment.

"Mum," said Ivy with a sigh. The subject of Ivy's failed prospects was not one she enjoyed revisiting.

"Everything!" her mother went on, gesticulating widely. "You'd have your Masters by now. You'd be an architect like you always dreamed! And what? What now? You're an unemployed sales rep. I had to watch him take everything from you, and now I have to watch him break your heart too."

Ivy gritted her teeth. "I am sorry this is so hard for YOU, Mum."

Her mother looked suddenly ashamed. "Oh Ivy," she said after a moment. "I'm sorry."

Ivy thawed. "It's okay." She wasn't actually angry with her mother. She was just hurting so fucking much that carrying anybody else's pain on top of her own was a request too much.

"No, it isn't," she said, reaching over and taking Ivy's hand again. "You're right."

"Thank you," said Ivy, giving her mother's hand a squeeze.

"Drink your prosecco." Said Emmeline.

"Yes, Mum."

Ivy drank then they sat in silence for a moment. She wasn't sure if the prosecco was making things better or worse, but she kept sipping it anyway. She was already down the rabbit hole.

"Have you had a good cry yet?" her mother asked after a moment.

"Mya and Julia got me rat-arsed on vodka last night," she said. "I cried, I screamed, I threw things."

"Good," said her mum with an approving nod. "You need to let it out. It's not healthy to squash it down."

Ivy nodded as her mother refilled her glass again. "There was no squashing," she said. "Believe me."

"Your father's going to do his nut, you know."

"Yep," said Ivy. "I know."

"Are you going to get a new job?"

"I'll have to," said Ivy. *Eurgh. Interviews.* Trying to pretend she was passionate about something she couldn't care less about. Meeting another grey wash of people in a bland office. Super. She took another sip of prosecco.

"You should go back to school," said her mother after a moment, looking at Ivy cautiously. This was not a new subject.

"Mum..."

"Too soon?"

"Too soon," agreed Ivy.

Emmeline nodded and reached over the table to put a hand gently on Ivy's cheek. "He'll be back."

"You think?"

"You're the most incredible woman, Ivy Reynolds," said her mother. "You're kind, smart, compassionate, and - luckily - you got your mother's looks."

Ivy smiled. "Thanks, Mum," she said, smiling sadly.

Her mother's face took on a sad, wistful expression. "I wish I'd been able to have more babies. It's one of my biggest regrets that everything happened the way it did. The world needs more people like you."

Ivy wiped tears from her eyes. She was already an emotional bomb just waiting to go off. Her mother's pride in her, despite her failed relationship and rubbish career prospects was just about the right amount to tip her over. Thinking of the children her mother had conceived and lost, remembering the heartbreak she had seen her experience but been too young to comprehend, was just too much.

"I'm so sorry, Mum," Ivy whispered, tears starting to trickle down her cheeks.

"Come now," said her mother, fishing what was almost certainly a used tissue out of her bra and dabbing Ivy's cheeks with it. "There's time for this later. For now, we shall focus on better things."

"What things?"

"Prosecco of course," said her mother, smiling mischievously. "And when he comes crawling back after realising what a complete shit he is, you can make him support you while you go back to school, like you supported him."

Ivy rolled her eyes. "Still too soon."

The waitress approached again, somewhat hesitantly this time. "Are we ready to order?"

"Another bottle of prosecco please!" said Ivy's mother with a goofy grin.

This was it. *This* was how Ivy was going to die. Face down on a restaurant table, surrounded by empty prosecco bottles and her mother's earrings.

Chapter Six

Ivy's head was banging. The prosecco was losing a battle to the vodka and wine from the night before and she was suffering the consequences.

After eventually escaping from her mother, Ivy had weaved her way home, and collapsed on the sofa. Three hours later she'd woken up, made herself a somewhat unappealing sandwich, and taken some very ineffective paracetamol. Now she sat staring at the uneaten sandwich, the TV blaring some game show she had no idea of the rules for and no inclination to care, and she was numb to everything except the hangover that was consuming her body.

Although the hangover was a revolting feeling, sort of like mould mixed with slug slime and somebody else's sweaty shoe, it was preferable to everything she'd been feeling before.

Ivy stared at the sandwich as it sat on the plate congealing slowly while the game show changed to a documentary about Nazis. Why had she made it? She wasn't hungry. She wasn't going to eat that stupid sandwich with its tired lettuce leaves and leftover cheese. Why bother pretending? What was the point? There was nobody there to care if she ate. Nobody there to care if she lived.

Feeling herself getting lost to melodrama, and overcome with the desperate urge to vomit, Ivy staggered away from the sofa and into the bathroom where she threw up the entire risotto she'd forced down at lunchtime.

Christ, that was disgusting. But, all things considered, it could have been worse.

She slid to the floor and pulled her phone out of her pocket. The screen was lit with tons of little green messages. Her mother; Mya and Julia sending thoughts of love and support, and the occasional threat of violence; Helen from her old work asking what her plans were and whether she had had the most magical birthday weekend ever. But nothing from Steven. Not a single text.

She opened her WhatsApp and, ignoring all the messages from everyone else, opened her chat with Steven. He hadn't been online since he'd phoned her at Carmelle's. It was as if he had vanished off the face of the earth. No social media updates, no retweets about rugby or politics, no hint of where he could be. For all she knew he'd left the country. For all she knew he'd died; consumed with grief and guilt about what he'd done to his beautiful wife, he had thrown himself from a railway bridge...

She was spiralling. She had to stop. She rubbed her eyes and forced the image of Steven's bloody and contorted body out of her mind. For one thing, if he'd felt that guilty, he'd just have come home and begged forgiveness. Which he hadn't. So he clearly didn't give a shit.

After deciding she was too old to sleep on the bathroom floor, she crawled to her feet, flushed the toilet, brushed her teeth and ditched the brush in the bin. Too gross.

Supporting herself on the wall, cursing her poor decision-making and wondering if it was true that hangovers last a whole week when you hit your thirties, Ivy made her way to the bedroom.

But she stopped, her hand on the door handle, frozen. Their bedroom. She hadn't been in. Not since he left. The idea had sent her into an absolute emotional cess pit earlier,

so Mya and Julia had fetched her clothes and carefully
shielded her from having to look inside. But now they
weren't here. And neither was Steven.

She took her hand away and took a deep breath. Their
bedroom.

The bedroom where she and Steven had made love.
Where they had dressed before work each morning,
cuddled in bed each night. The room he had burst into,
singing Build Me Up Buttercup, at 5am, after he'd set his
clock wrong and thought it was 8am and he was being
romantic. Where they'd decided that as they were up so
early anyway, they'd walk to the park to watch the sunrise
over the lake. The room where they'd lain side by side,
staring into each other's eyes, and wistfully making plans,
shaping a future together with a home and a dog, three
children, and holidays to Spain in the six weeks off school.
Where they'd dreamed of what it would look like when
they were REAL adults.

She couldn't stand there forever. For one thing, she was
so dizzy she'd probably fall on her face if she didn't lie
down soon. She pushed open the door and went inside.

The light from the moon and the streetlamp over the
street cut streaks across the room. It looked almost the
same, the absence almost imperceptible if you didn't know
what you were looking for. Most of the decoration and
softness of the room came from her own things; he was
minimal in his approach to decoration. But Ivy could see
the changes; she could feel the changes. Despite being full
of her own belongings, the room felt empty.

She walked into the room and looked around slowly.

Her dresser was there - make up, perfumes, jewellery,
her to-be-read pile that teetered up high. Then there was
his. A screwed-up tissue sat alone. He hadn't even bothered

to bin his snot. *How hastily do you have to be running away from the home you share with your wife to not even bother to take three seconds to bin your own snot?*

She opened the wardrobe doors and looked inside. One side was full of brightly coloured cardigans, dresses and shirts. The other side was bare, except for empty hangers.

And a scarf.

On the floor of the wardrobe lay a dropped and forgotten-about black and grey striped scarf. Abandoned. Left behind. Not important enough to warrant returning for.

Ivy picked up the scarf and fingered the fine knit. He'd worn that scarf a lot in the winter just gone. A gift from an uncle for Christmas, she remembered, and just the right, sensible style to compliment his business-like work demeanour. A forgotten scarf, left all alone, by the person who'd loved it so much before.

Ivy buried her face in that scarf and sniffed. Dior Sauvage was ingrained into the weave, even though it had been months since it had been worn. She held it close, closing her eyes, letting that smell send her back into his arms, back into their life together.

The smell of Steven's neck. The neck she had kissed, the neck she had helped him adjust a tie around. The neck she had swung her arms around as they'd danced on their wedding night, twirling and laughing, so full of joy and love. The neck she had rested her cheek against as they'd swayed together, her long white dress sweeping across the floor as she counted all the ways she was blessed to be marrying this wonderful, smart and handsome man who had chosen her to be his wife.

Ivy's knees buckled. Her throat gasped. Her eyes burned. She fell to her knees, the scarf pressed to her face, and sobbed for every single dream she had lost. Every idea for the future, every plan, every hope. In a single moment, they had been stolen from her, snatched away as if that whole life she was excited to lead had never existed at all, and she had been left with nothing but an unwanted scarf to remember them by.

***

Ivy woke up on the floor of the bedroom.

"Shit," she grumbled.

In her youth, Ivy had been known to pass out on many a floor during parties or sleepovers. She'd slept under tables; she'd slept behind sofas, and she'd slept in a friend's kitchen sink once, but she'd been young and, for the most part, her body had wriggled back into the correct shape incredibly quickly.

Times had changed. She tried to straighten her spine and groaned in pain as something cracked and all her muscles seemed to seize up.

So far, being thirty sucked.

She couldn't live on the floor. She had to get up. Forcing herself to her feet, Ivy stood up and rubbed her back, digging her fingers into the sore knots that had coiled up below her skin. Looking down, she saw the scarf. The black and grey scarf soaked in tears and Steven's perfume, just lying there in a heap, abandoned once again. She went to pick it up but changed her mind. For now, it could stay put.

Staggering out of the bedroom and into the living room, Ivy saw the TV still playing from the night before, her abandoned sandwich festering on the table looking even more pitiful than she remembered. She turned off the TV and carried the sandwich into the kitchen, tipped it into the bin and dumped the plate in the sink.

What was she supposed to do? She had no job to go to. No husband to chat to. It was just so silent, so still.

What did she normally do on a day off? She'd had days off without Steven there before. She'd been alone in the house without him on numerous occasions. Yet now everything felt cold and stiff, like she was in a vacuum. Like Steven had taken all the air with him when he left.

Ivy shivered and started making coffee. Coffee was job one. Coffee would help.

She put the kettle on to boil, fetched an Eeyore mug from the cupboard and the tub of coffee from the shelf. As she went to pour the water onto the grounds, she heard something rattle the door. She looked up sharply. Post man? Mya coming to visit with yet more vodka? She hoped not - she'd probably die.

Stepping out of the kitchen and into the living room, Ivy saw the front door opening. Her breath caught in her throat. It couldn't be...?

"Steven!" she gasped, as her husband stepped into the room, framed by the bright morning light, bringing waves of fresh air into the room.

She stared at him. He was back! Julia and her mother had said he'd come back and they were right! She took a deep breath.

"Hello," said Steven, closing the door behind him and plunging the room back into darkness.

Ivy stared at him. Studied him. His dark curls, his crooked nose, the scar on his chin from where a dog had bitten him as a child. The face she knew so well. Oh how she loved that face! She stepped towards him, her arms out ready to hold him and forgive him and pretend none of this had ever happened, ready to smell that neck again.

Steven stepped backwards. "I didn't come for that," he said coldly.

"For what?" she whispered, her heart sinking.

"To... reconcile," he said.

Ivy felt herself tighten. She felt angry. "I don't know if it counts as a reconciliation if you've not had a fight and you've been apart less than 48 hours."

"Well, whatever," said Steven, irritated by her snark. He was always irritated by her snark. It did nothing to make her feel less like being snarky. "Can we sit?"

"It's your house," said Ivy, gesturing to the sofa.

"Yes," said Steven, walking stiffly past her, and sitting down, leaning his elbows on his knees. "It is."

Ivy sat opposite him. She looked at him, waiting. He looked tired. They sat in silence. Ivy's head was fuzzy, and she thought wistfully of the coffee she'd been about to make. He still said nothing, just chewed on his lip looking thoughtful.

Despite her anger, Ivy felt a sense of awkward hope.

"Would you like a drink?" she said after a moment. She wanted coffee; Steven loved coffee. And maybe a sense of domestic normalcy would help. "I was about to make coffee."

"No," he said, awkwardly. "Thanks."

"Are you sure?" she said, standing up. "It's tense as all hell in here and we've got that delicious Columbian stuff in, and I was literally just making some when you came home so it's really no bother, and maybe some caffeine would..."

"I said no, Ivy," he said.

"Well, maybe I'll get some," said Ivy, waving her arms and feeling like an idiot but not knowing how to stop. "Caffeine always helps me think and it's not like we're saying anything in here for me to miss..."

"Ivy!" snapped Steven, looking up at her. "Stop!"

Ivy looked at him. His tone was like a slap in the face. She sat down heavily, trying to decide whether she needed to cry over him or shout at him. She knew she was rambling, awkwardly blathering on because she couldn't focus her thoughts enough to say anything sensible, but still... it hurt.

They went back to silence. Ivy trembling with emotions that threatened to overwhelm her. Condemned to wait on Steven's decision about when, and if, he was going to speak for fear of being shouted at again.

Finally, he looked up at her, meeting her eye with a serious look.

"Our marriage is over, Ivy," he said firmly. "I've moved out. For good."

She opened her mouth then closed it again. What was she supposed to say? What was he expecting? She couldn't think of any words, not even a ramble. All she could hear in her head was a loud buzzing sound.

"You need to understand that I will not be paying the rent on this house anymore," he went on, his voice tainted with patronising condescension. "I need to find my own home to start over in."

He was speaking to her like she was a naughty child who didn't understand why drawing on the walls was wrong. She felt herself wanting to pick up the candlestick from the coffee table and hurl it at him.

"Now, I realise that the rent and bills on this house are above your income bracket," he said, sounding evermore twatty, "but we need to be grown-ups about this. You might need to consider working harder to get a better job."

Ivy's fingernails dug into her thighs. It was a really good job she wasn't holding that coffee. "Work harder?" she whispered quietly, the anger bubbling furiously in her guts.

"Or, if you prefer, perhaps take on an extra evening or weekend job, something more at your level," he said.

"Because an evening or weekend job... at my level... would bring in the equivalent of a doctor's salary?"

Steven looked irritated. He leaned back against the sofa and folded his arms huffily. "There is no need to be sarcastic, Ivy," he said. "I'm trying to help you."

"Oh, I'm so sorry," said Ivy, her hand to her chest in mock humility. "I didn't notice!"

Steven sighed and stood up. "Forget it. I thought we could be mature enough to have an adult conversation about how to move on amicably from this relationship."

Ivy's fury became volcanic.

"Mature?" Ivy cried, standing up herself and staring at him with red hot rage. "Amicably move on? You absolute thundercunt! You moved out in secret! On my birthday! And told me over the phone while I was in public! You think THAT was mature, do you, Steven? You think THAT was the absolute most mature and grown-up way of handling this?"

"Ivy..." said Steven. But Ivy was on a roll.

"You think ending your marriage while I was getting ready to go to the surprise birthday party, filled with my friends and family, which, by the way, YOU fucking arranged!" she was getting louder now; and Steven glanced at the walls, embarrassed. Let the neighbours hear, she thought, it's not like he was going to be around to deal with the consequences. "Plus, Steven, it was also the day I lost

my lowly job! Just to emphasise how good your timing is!
You've really nailed the art of kicking a girl when she's
down, Steven!"

"Ivy," said Steven, sounding angry. Fuck him. He had
no right to be angry. This was his doing! This was all his
doing! And she wasn't going to let him interrupt her. He'd
had his go. There was more to say.

"But you're right! Of course, you're right. I've had
nearly forty-eight hours to process the emotional fall out of
my five-year marriage coming to an unexpected end! I
should be more mature. Just like you! You are the beacon of
maturity, Steven Rhodes, a shining example of how to
behave like a grown up. The mature man who can't even
face the woman he married to tell her he's leaving or why!"

Steven turned and headed for the door. Ivy felt tears of
rage and despair start to pour down her cheeks. Hot tears
that splashed heavily.

"Oh! Are you leaving Steven? How very unexpected! I
never realised having a difficult conversation was too hard
for such a mature person to handle! Please! Teach me how
to behave like such an adult!"

Steven opened the door and turned to Ivy, the image of
calm against her wild-eyed rage, and seeming smug about
it. "My lawyer will be arranging the transfer of the house
into your name tomorrow," he said. "Goodbye, Ivy."

Steven turned from her and closed the door.

Ivy threw back her head and screamed.

Chapter Seven

Ivy sat in her car outside her mother's house. Every so often she put her hand on the door handle. Then she took it off again.

Hand on the door handle. Off again.

Did she really have to move home?

She had no income. She had no partner. She had no home.

She'd phoned the landlord, explained the situation, and agreed to terminate their contract immediately. He'd been relatively understanding, but she could tell her explanation and emotional despair didn't interest him. But at least it was done. After that she'd just needed to get out. She couldn't handle being in that space for any longer than necessary. It might have been in her name, but it wasn't hers. It never had been really. It had always been his.

Most of her belongings were in binbags; she'd filled them with clothes and furnishings and memories. She had piled books into suitcases and kitchenware into boxes that had once housed the vacuum cleaner and the kettle, and which Steven had insisted on keeping.

She had carefully opened the cabinet in the living room where a tiny matchstick house lived. It was the first house she'd ever built. She'd been six years old and determined that she was going to build people's dream houses so they could always be happy and safe with their families. It had moved everywhere she had, a strange and sad reminder that she didn't build houses, not even boring ones, but a precious keepsake from a time when she'd believed she could. Steven had thought it was ugly and it had been stashed out of sight in the cupboard since they'd moved in together. Now it was wrapped in layers of kitchen paper and sitting nestled in her handbag, coming home to the house where it was built.

Ivy put her head back and closed her eyes. She hadn't lived with her parents since university. But what choice did she have? She was lucky she had them there.

She put her head on the steering wheel. This was so fucking horrible. She was in so much pain. She could barely breathe if she let herself think about it.

After a few minutes she heard a tapping on the window next to her. Ivy turned her head and saw her mother looking at her curiously.

Ivy wound down the window.

"Hello, Mum," she said.

"Why are you lurking out here?" asked her mother.

"I'm thirty. Unemployed. My husband left me. And now I'm homeless."

Her mum took a second to process this new revelation of Ivy's ever-spiralling life, then looked over her shoulder. "ROBERT!" she shouted. "GET THE BAILEYS!"

Ivy heard from somewhere inside the house, "Yes, dear!"

Ivy got out of the car and her mother pulled her into a tight hug. "You're going to be okay, Ivy," she said to her. "I promise."

"I'm not," she said. "But thank you."

"You are one day," said her mother. "And I'm going to be here while we wait."

Ivy started to cry. Her mother held her closely, making soothing noises Ivy remembered from childhood. From hurting her knees, from failing exams, from falling out with friends. She remembered feeling like those were life-changing, devastating pains, but looking back she'd take them a thousand times over rather than this. She cried heavily into her mother's pale blue cashmere sweater, leaving an impressive slug trail of snot which her mum noticed but said nothing about. She just kept making gentle shushing sounds and stroking her daughter's hair.

"Erm," came Ivy's father's voice behind them. "Em?"

"Get her cases out of her car, Robert," said Emmeline, putting an arm around Ivy's shoulders as they headed into the house.

"What's going on?" he asked.

"The scoundrel has added making her homeless to his list of crimes," she said as she led Ivy towards the house.

"Oh, bloody hell," said Robert.

In the kitchen, Ivy sat down heavily at the kitchen table.

"You can stay here for as long as you need," said her mother as she poured Baileys into glasses and set one down in front of Ivy.

"The Gilmores are staying this weekend," said Ivy's father, coming in with a suitcase and resting it against the wall.

Emmeline flapped a hand at him with a stern glare, "You, shush," she instructed, before turning back to Ivy. "You are ALWAYS welcome here."

Ivy sipped her Baileys with a sad but grateful smile. "I won't stay long... I just need to..."

"Figure out what you're doing with your life?" interjected Emmeline.

"Yeah."

"And get a new job," said her father from the doorway.

"Sure."

"She should go back to school," Emmeline argued.

"She's thirty years old!" said Ivy's dad incredulously. "What's she going to do at a school?"

"Not a children's school, you fool," said Emmeline crossly. "University or college! She should never have dropped out of education in the first place."

Ivy picked up the Baileys bottle and refilled her glass.

"But then what is she going to do for money?" asked Ivy's father, hands on his hips.

"She'll live here!" said Emmeline, as if he was stupid.

"For the length of a degree?!" Ivy's father looked aghast.

Ivy drank more Baileys.

"Yes, Robert," said Emmeline through gritted teeth. "For the length of a degree. Or longer. Because she's our daughter and she *needs* us. Do you have a problem with that?"

"It's a bloody good job we only had the one," said Robert as he stomped out of the door muttering to himself. "They're not cheap to keep!"

"So," said Emmeline, turning back to Ivy. "A degree."

"Mum?" Ivy interrupted. "Can we talk about this another time? Please?"

Ivy's mum checked herself and nodded apologetically. "Of course, darling," she said. "I'm so sorry. I was rushing ahead again."

"Just a tad," said Ivy, sipping more Baileys.

Her father came back in with two more cases. "Is this everything?" he asked.

"No," said Ivy. "The rest is still in the house but it's all packed. I've got a week to get it all out."

"Where's it going to go?" asked her father, looking at the pile of things in the kitchen. "Your bedroom isn't big enough to fit an entire house in!"

"She'll put most of it in the garage," said Emmeline. "Obviously."

"The garage!" protested Robert. "But..."

"Yes?" asked Emmeline, her eyes flashing. "Where else do you propose we keep her things? The dining room? The bathroom?"

"A storage unit," said Robert. "She could rent one over in the unit on Beaconside."

"Nonsense," said Emmeline. "She's got no income to rent a storage unit or she'd be able to rent a house. And the garage is free."

Ivy rested her head on the table. She loved her parents very much, but their bickering was wearing at the best of times.

"Now look, you've upset Ivy," said Emmeline, reaching over and putting a protective hand on her daughter's back.

"The garage is fine," said Robert gruffly. "I'll take the trailer over in the week and get everything else out."

"Thanks, Dad," Ivy said into the tabletop. "I appreciate that.

"Don't mention it, darling," her mother said. "Now, what would you like for lunch?"

"I'm not really hungry," said Ivy.

"Nonsense," said Robert. "A good hot meal is just what you need. You never did cope well without a belly full of food."

"I agree," said Emmeline, nodding wisely to her husband. "A good old-fashioned family Sunday lunch is exactly what she needs."

Ivy sighed. There was no point arguing.

"I think there's a chicken in the freezer!" said Robert eagerly, heading across the room, seemingly glad he could do something to help.

"Erm, Dad," said Ivy. "I'm vegetarian..."

"Since when?" asked her father, looking baffled.

Ivy sighed. "Since I was fifteen, Dad."

"Oh," said Robert. "Right. Of course. I think we have some carrots."

"She eats more than just carrots," said Emmeline. "Honestly, Robert!"

"I swear she used to eat meat."

"She did! When she was fourteen!"

"No, she's eaten meat since."

"I haven't, Dad."

"Are you sure? Wasn't there chicken at the wedding?"

"Yes, but I didn't eat it," said Ivy.

"I see," said her father, looking thoroughly bemused by the entire situation.

Ivy sighed again. She felt like she was going to sigh heavily a lot until she could afford to move out.

Ivy's mother rolled her eyes. "Ivy, darling," she said. "Why don't you take your bags upstairs and get yourself settled, wash your face and freshen yourself up, then you can come downstairs and peel some potatoes for me."

"Yes, Mum."

Ivy downed the last of her Baileys, and stood up, picked up her main suitcase and obediently went up to her bedroom. Because that is what it was now. Her room. The only space she had that was her own.

Last time she'd stayed overnight there had been Christmas the previous year. She and Steven had lain under the McFly poster in the flowery bed and stared up at the ceiling, giggling because of all the sherry and groaning because they were so full of food, and talked about Christmases they'd had as children and how one day they'd like to see Christmas in New York.

Ivy welled up at the memory. Christmas in New York would never happen now. All her ideas of them walking around Central Park in the snow, ice skating at Rockefeller Centre, eating hot pretzels from a street vendor and watching the steam rise up through the icy air... gone.

She pushed open the bedroom door and went inside. It was still the same, but now with the added exercise bike her father had bought at a car-boot sale, much to her mother's bemusement, that they were now apparently using to dry laundry on.

She pushed the exercise bike against the wall, swung her suitcase onto the bed, and took it all in. Ten minutes after moving back into her parent's house and she was fifteen years old again: her parents leaving her exasperated by their efforts to control her life; feeling overwhelmed by more emotions than she knew how to cope with, and about to go and help her mother in the kitchen, listening to Dolly Parton singing and her father complaining about it.

Sitting down on the floral duvet cover, she took out her phone and scrolled through the messages. Mya and Julia sending love and concern, offering different suggestions on how to cope (Mya highly in favour of alcohol, Julia suggesting yoga), and one from her former landlord informing her that she wouldn't be getting the security deposit back. *Fucking marvellous.*

"Ivy!" came her mother's voice from downstairs. "Are you feeling more Meatloaf or Dolly today?"

Ivy rolled her eyes. "Dolly, Mum," she called. "When in doubt, always Dolly!"

"Fuck's sake," she heard her dad complain as 'Love Is Like A Butterfly' started blasting out of the Alexa. She could practically see her mother's triumphant face.

Standing up, Ivy embraced her fate and headed downstairs.

Chapter Eight

Ivy checked the time on her phone. Midnight. It was officially Monday. Her first unemployed Monday. The first day of the rest of her life and she was looking up at a picture of Harry Judd and smelling the passion fruit scented fabric softener her mother had used for as long as she remembered.

Her mind started doing mental calculations about how much sleep she'd get if she finally got to sleep now, but then she stopped. Did it matter? She didn't have to set an alarm for 7AM. She didn't have to get up, shower, pack a lunch and get to work on time. She didn't have to do anything. She could stay in bed all day if she wanted. Nothing mattered anymore.

She felt like it should be liberating but it wasn't. Normally, the freedom of not having any responsibility came with the bonus of being on holiday. It was a novelty, a rare treat, and to be revelled in. But this didn't feel like the first day of a holiday. This was the first day of being so unimportant and insignificant that nobody expected anything of her at all. Even her friends would be too busy to care if she got up or not. Mya would be busy on some set, making actors looking fabulous, and Julia would be presenting some compelling argument about why her firm should work with some rich capitalist. When 9am rolled around, her state of existence would mean literally nothing to anybody.

She rolled over and stared into the darkness.

She wondered what Steven was doing. Was he awake? Was he thinking about her? She could call the hospital and ask to speak to him. She could just go and wait outside to catch him as he came or left.

Was that creepy stalker behaviour? If she'd been a single woman hoping for a date then definitely yes. But she was his wife! Was it still creepy?

What if she saw him with another woman? Oh God...!

Her stomach dropped.

She couldn't cope with that.

Rolling over, Ivy tried to force the image out of her head. She stared at the wall. She counted the spots on the wallpaper, picked at her thumbnail, and tried to ignore the churning in her guts. Ultimately, she knew she was too scared to go and confront him, even if he wasn't with another woman. Not because she was too scared to talk to him - there were so many things she wanted to say that speaking to him would come easily. She was scared of facing his rejection for the third time in less than a week.

Eventually exhaustion dominated her and she fell asleep. A restless, disturbed sleep, but being unconscious for at least some of the time was less painful than being awake, so she accepted it.

The next morning, Ivy heard movement downstairs and was lured to her feet by the smell of fresh coffee. She stumbled out of the room, stubbing her toe on the exercise bike on her way out, and headed for the stairs.

In the kitchen she found her mother dressed smartly at the table, eating a piece of toast and marmalade, and drinking coffee whilst she read the paper.

"Good morning, sunshine," she said, looking up at Ivy with a smile.

Ivy, her hair in an intense state of disarray, and the solid hour and a half of sleep leaving dirty grey bags under her eyes, did not feel like sunshine. If weather nicknames were called for, she was the kind of dismal sleet that formed brown sludge by mingling with the mud on the ground. But she didn't comment. She just grunted and shuffled towards the coffee pot and poured herself a big mug full.

"What are you doing today?" Emmeline asked her as Ivy sat down at the table, rubbing her eyes.

Ivy shrugged.

"I see your communication skills have regressed to the standards of last time you lived here," her mother observed, with eyebrows raised.

Ivy glared at her over the mug of coffee. Cracks about her lack of maturity were not going to go down well for a long time yet.

"I dunno," said Ivy after a moment.

"Well, if you want my advice, you need to take some time to process and heal," said her mother. "Then you can start to figure out what it is you want from your life, and then work out how to get it."

"Whatever," Ivy grumbled. She was not in the mood for a pep talk.

What did she want? Her old life back, her husband, her home? Even her stupid job at this point would be a step up from what she had now. She wanted to go back to being 29, back to before her world fell apart. And how to get it? She couldn't. It was over. Everything she wanted was gone and she couldn't do anything about it.

Emmeline sighed, finished the last corner of toast and put her cup and plate in the sink, before kissing Ivy on the head.

"I'm off to work," she said. "There's no pressure, alright, sweetheart? Take as long as you need. But when you're ready, we WILL get your life back on track. I promise you."

"Yes, Mum," said Ivy.

As it turned out, what Ivy wanted that day was to eat Doritos and binge watch Gossip Girl. So, that was what she did.

She ignored phone calls from Helen at her old job, she ignored a text from Cousin Hayley expressing shock and dismay at Ivy's current predicament, and she ignored every single social media notification because she couldn't bear to see if her relationship status had been changed, or if she and Steven were still even friends at all. Gossip Girl and Doritos. That was her life now. That, and a rather excellently thick blanket she found in the airing cupboard and decided she would live in for the rest of time.

When her mother arrived home, she picked half a Dorito out of Ivy's hair and tossed it in the bin, turned off the TV, and led Ivy into the kitchen.

Ivy sat down heavily at the table as Emmeline poured them both a glass of red wine.

"Dolly or Dusty?" she asked.

"Dusty," said Ivy.

Emmeline nodded and commanded Alexa to play 'It Begins Again.'

Dusty's voice rang out, full of sorrow. *"I'd rather leave while I'm still in love, while I still believe in the meaning of the word. I'll keep my dreams and just pretend, that you and I were never meant to end."*

Ivy took a deep drink of her wine. *Fuck. My. Life.*

Emmeline started gathering vegetables to get on with dinner, humming along and pretending not to notice the agony of the song choice. Probably deciding that calling attention to it would only make it worse. She chopped some peppers then fetched some tomatoes from the fridge, glancing over at Ivy every so often.

"Daddy's out with the chaps from the squash club this evening, so it's just us girls," she said, with artificially cheeriness after a moment.

"Great," said Ivy, her artificial cheeriness lacking the enthusiasm of her mother's.

"I'm going to make us a nice ratatouille," said her mother, fetching a large pot from the cupboard and popping it down smartly on the stove top. "And I thought we could watch a nice movie!"

Nice. Her mother was saying nice a lot which meant she was floundering. She always ran out of interesting adjectives when she was struggling to maintain positivity.

"I'm not really in the mood, Mum," said Ivy, glumly. "But thanks."

Emmeline carried on, pretending she hadn't heard Ivy.

"Would you prefer rice or pasta?"

"I don't know," grumbled Ivy.

"How about rice," said her mum, nodding. "Rice is nice."

"I guess," said Ivy.

"And I've bought us a lovely lemon cheesecake for pudding," she said, side-eying Ivy.

Ivy hesitated and chewed her lip. "I'll take the cheesecake," she said after a moment.

"Not without some dinner first you won't, young lady," said her mother, chopping up an onion.

"I'm thirty years old, mother," said Ivy grumpily. "I can decide what I eat for dinner."

"Well, in my house, if you want cheesecake, you eat dinner first," said Emmeline. "And you eat cheesecake whilst watching a film with your mother."

Ivy eyeballed her. "Fine."

"Good girl," said her mother. "Now, why don't you be a sweetheart and come and make the rice for me while I do this."

Ivy sighed as Dusty sang, "I got so much to share, so much to care for, 'cause darlin' I found love with you."

Ivy downed her wine. She should have picked Dolly. At least Dolly hated that Jolene bitch. Ivy stood up and retrieved the rice from the cupboard, picked up the bottle of wine off the side and took a deep swing from the neck.

"Oh Ivy!" said her mother horrified. "Don't be disgusting! That is SO uncouth."

Ivy put the bottle down on the side and got on with making the rice, grumping "Uncouth," to herself irritably.

"So," said her mother as Ivy poured the rice into a pan. "How was your first day off?"

"It wasn't a day off," snapped Ivy. "It's only a day off if you're going to have a day on again." She was aware that she was being more irritable with her mother than she deserved, but she felt far too grouchy to turn it off.

Her mother looked at her with a side eye. She looked like she was hurt but trying not to show it, and Ivy immediately felt ashamed of herself. "How was your first day of unemployment?" she asked.

"I found an excellent blanket," said Ivy, forcing herself to be nicer. It wasn't her mother's fault she was in such a foul mood. "That was nice."

"Ah, I saw you were bundled in that," said her mother, nodding, a natural smile returning to her face. "I bought that at Boundary Mill in the sale, you know."

"Oh right," said Ivy, pouring the water onto the rice.

"I bumped into Marjorie when I was there," her mother went on merrily. "You remember Marjorie, don't you?"

"Not really," said Ivy.

"Yes, you do!" insisted Emmeline, tossing chopped peppers into her sizzling pan of onions. "You went to school with her daughter, Caroline!"

"I don't know anyone called Caroline," said Ivy. These conversations with her mother had been a staple of her childhood. It was almost nostalgic.

"Oh," said her mother thoughtfully. "I was sure she said it was Caroline. Maybe it was Constance. Cathy? Her surname's Partridge."

"Charlotte?"

"Yes! Charlotte Partridge!" said her mother, gesticulating triumphantly with her wooden spoon, flicking hot tomato juice onto Ivy's pyjamas. "That's the one. I knew there was a C in there. She's a surgeon now, did you know that?"

"Nope," said Ivy, pouring wine into her glass.

"Marjorie's ever so proud," Emmeline went on.

Ivy drank her wine.

"You should text her," said Emmeline, glancing sideways.

"Why?" asked Ivy.

"Just... to catch up."

"I can't catch success, mother," said Ivy, feeling her bad mood returning. "It doesn't transfer via osmosis. Anyway, if it did, Julia would have rubbed herself all over my body years ago."

"I'm just..."

"And remember the man I am technically still married to? The SURGEON?"

Her mother's eyes darkened. "Yes."

"If proximity to highly qualified medical professionals were to have some kind of magical power don't you think it would have happened by now?"

Emmeline sighed. "Fine, you're right," she said.

"I'll get there when I'm ready," said Ivy.

Emmeline put a hand on Ivy's cheek. "I know you will, darling. I just want you to have a beautiful life."

"I know, Mum."

"And I know how smart you are."

"I know, Mum."

"And I'm your mother and I'm programmed to worry about you."

"I know, Mum."

"Drink your wine. It'll help drown me out."

"Yes, Mum."

"You break me, shake me, yeah, I ain't movin' backwards. Shake me, take me, yeah, I keep on goin'." Dusty sang.

Ivy narrowed her eyes at the Alexa. She was starting to feel personally attacked.

***

Ivy woke up in the living room in the dark. A half-eaten piece of cheesecake was on a plate on her lap, and she was still wrapped in the Boundary Mill blanket. Her mother was nowhere to be seen.

Ivy checked the time on her phone. It was 2AM. Apparently the film had not captured her attention. Or, given the headache rumbling around the back of her eyeballs, perhaps the red wine had got the better of her.

Stretching, Ivy considered getting up and going to bed, but she changed her mind. Fuck it. Might as well stay here. She ate the last of the cheesecake, then lay back down and went to sleep.

She was woken in the morning by her father tapping her sharply on the head with a rolled-up newspaper.

"Hey!" she protested, flailing her arms around

"I like to read the paper on the sofa before work," he said, standing over her with a pointed look on his face.

"Sit on the armchair!" she protested.

"I sit on the sofa in the morning," he said, not moving. "I put my coffee on the windowsill, and my feet up on that stool. If I sit on the armchair then I have no windowsill and no stool."

"The stools not nailed down, Dad," Ivy grumbled. "Just move it over to the bloody armchair."

"You want me to rip the window frame out too, I suppose?" he asked.

"For God's sake, Dad!" protested Ivy, but her father still didn't move, so Ivy sighed dramatically and forced herself out from the fluffy cocoon. Before she had even fully stood up, her father dropped into the seat. Possibly concerned she'd change her mind.

Ivy rolled her eyes and headed upstairs. She heard her father sigh in satisfaction as his feet landed on the stool and his coffee landed on the windowsill, then the flap of the newspaper opening up.

Trudging upstairs, Ivy wondered how long she'd be able to cope living in this weird purgatory between adulthood and childhood, whether she'd lose her mind, and whether she'd left any Doritos in her bedroom. She'd find that out soon enough, at least.

Alas. No Doritos.

Ivy lay face down on her bed and wondered if life was even worth living. No husband. No home. No job. And now no Doritos.

Chapter Nine

The days gradually drifted by. Soon they were weeks. Ivy found herself losing track of time, losing track of her thoughts. She braved the world of social media and confirmed that Steven had indeed ended their relationship on Facebook and subsequently blocked her from stalking his profile.

She found her inbox filled with a mix of well-wishers and grief junkies, crying out for the gory details of the break-up amid concern for her well-being. She saw multiple erect and ugly penises - some from complete strangers, and one from a married pastor from the Church she'd once attended for a friend's wedding. Ivy growled.

On more than one occasion she deleted the Facebook app off her phone, but it didn't last. She considered setting up a fake profile with a fake photo and attempting some surreptitious stalking. Could she be that petty? Yes, of course she could. But she was also too scared of getting caught out, so she held off.

"He's blocked me too!" her mother exclaimed when Ivy told her, as she swooped on her phone to check it out.

"Well, yeah," said Ivy. "I'm not surprised. You're my mother."

"But he and I were friends!" she protested. "We got on so well!"

"He's a cretin," said Ivy's father. "How anybody could not want you two in their lives I don't know. He's obviously stupid."

Ivy put a hand to her heart, "Dad!" she whispered, moved by his sudden turn to sentimentality.

"Oh, don't get mushy, Ivy," he said, before hiding back behind his newspaper. But Ivy noted a small smile on his face.

"Probably worried I'll tell the world what an abandoning BASTARD he is," growled Emmeline.

"Yeah, probably," agreed Ivy.

Ivy's mother had muttered something about feeling betrayed and stomped off, but Ivy didn't have the energy to deal with her mother's sense of pain over Steven's abandonment. She was still struggling enough with her own.

She was still struggling at night too. She missed the sense of comfort and warmth she got from Steven's body being beside her own. She missed the fluff that crept up his lower back, which he hated and sometimes got waxed off, but she loved because it was so soft.

Sometimes she cried herself to sleep; sometimes she just lay flat and still, staring up at the ceiling in the darkness. Sometimes she fell asleep quickly but soon woke up after having dreams of either Steven's return, or reliving the moment he left over and over and over. Sometimes with spiders.

The restless nights left her lacking energy in the day, and she had soon binge watched her way through assorted glossy teen dramas on Netflix, and several documentary series about serial killers.

Mya and Julia came by regularly, usually armed with alcohol, which delighted Ivy's mother. Apparently getting drunk with friends was the appropriate response to trauma, and Emmeline found hosting these events to be thrilling. She started stocking junk food and wine for such occasions, and would welcome Mya and Julia with joy, throwing on Dolly or Dusty, and filling their glasses full. Ivy's father would usually excuse himself and go to the pub. Apparently too much oestrogen in the house was overwhelming.

"Steven is the most colossal twat," said Mya firmly on one such evening. It was a common theme for the conversations, between the usual work chat and catch ups.

"I quite agree," said Emmeline.

"I saw him," said Julia quietly, looking at her glass.

"What?" cried Ivy, Emmeline and Mya at once. "Where?"

"Just out," she said, shrugging nonchalantly, obviously feeling ashamed for not bringing it up sooner. "You know, walking. Around. Fred wanted to go and say hello."

"You didn't let him, did you!?" Ivy cried in horror, spilling wine on the table as she frantically leaned towards Julia.

"Of course not!" said Julia quickly. "But you know what he's like. He's all, 'Steven didn't leave us' about it. But I dragged him into a bakery and threatened to throw pork pies at him 'til he backed down."

"Good," said Ivy, sitting back with relief.

"I'd have punched him," muttered Mya.

"Fred or Steven?" asked Emmeline.

"Both," said Mya.

Emmeline clinked her glass against Mya's with an approving nod.

Playing with her wedding ring, Ivy asked, "Did he...look...okay?"

"Well, he was breathing," said Julia.

"Shame," grumbled Mya.

"You know something," said Ivy's mother, holding up her wine glass and sloshing a bit of Shiraz across the table. "That boy lied to me!"

"Excuse me?" asked Ivy.

"He lied to me!" said Emmeline again. "He promised me that he would look after you. PROMISED ME. I let him take my only daughter, my perfect baby girl, and I trusted him! I thought he was a bit of a knob for putting his career ahead of yours, but I actually loved that boy. I LOVED him! I trusted him. And I let him take my baby. I let him hurt you, Ivy. I always swore I would NEVER let anybody hurt you! And I am so very sorry."

Emmeline put a hand on Ivy's cheek and started to cry.

"Oh, Mum!" cried Ivy, taking her mother's hand.

Julia rubbed Emmeline's back. "It's not your fault," she said.

"Oh, I know," she said, sniffing fruitily and taking another drink. "Logically I know that. But I feel betrayed. Not just angry for you, Ivy, though I *am* obviously, more than anything. But I feel like he hurt me too, because he hurt the person I love most, after promising me he wouldn't."

Emmeline started crying a fresh wave of tears, and Ivy fell into her arms.

They cried together as Ivy's father opened the door and came in, shaking off his umbrella. When he noticed his wife and daughter sobbing drunkenly, he sighed heavily.

"Oh, bloody hell," he muttered. "What's happened now?"

"They're just having a moment, Mr Reynolds," said Julia.

"They're one big moment at the minute," he muttered to himself as he stomped through. "Tell Em I'll be upstairs."

After her father had left, Ivy broke away from her mother and sniffed.

"We should probably head off now," said Julia. "It's getting late."

"Are you going to be okay?" asked Mya.

"We'll be alright," said Emmeline. "Just got to get that stupid man out of our systems, that's all."

Julia and Mya stood and kissed them on the cheeks before heading out.

"I love you, Mum," said Ivy, finishing her wine.

"I love you too, Ivy," said Emmeline. "And we shouldn't waste another minute on that man. He's not worth it."

Ivy nodded sadly, "Yeah. You're right."

***

The next morning Ivy came downstairs, her head banging, and made a coffee. The light in the kitchen was too much so she carried the mug full of liquid-life into the living room and sat in the armchair, to avoid her father's stool and windowsill arrangement. Pulling the fluffy blanket around herself, she sipped her coffee and groaned in despair. She was too old for this hangover nonsense now. Her body couldn't cope.

In an effort to distract herself from the nausea that was growing in her gut, she took out her phone and redownloaded the Facebook app yet again.

"Oh, for the love of fuck," she muttered as she saw her inbox was loaded with messages.

She clicked to open it and saw that yet more randoms and weirdos of the internet had flocked to her, like moths to a very hungover flame. She wasn't in the mood. But if she didn't clear them out, they'd be waiting for her. Taking a solid glug of coffee, she went in.

Two men she went to high school with asking for dates - "you've grown into a woman!"; Barry from accounting at her former job, "I'm divorced too! Let's get together and share war stories... and maybe more!", and some kid who looked about nineteen with his wang out – "do u want cock babe?" She snarled at her phone and dumped it on the arm of chair. Fucking men.

Her father came shuffling in, newspaper under his arm, and coffee in his hands.

"Dad..." said Ivy, looking up and groaning. "Where're your trousers?"

"In the dryer," he said as he sat down and stretched his feet out to reach the footstool.

"Do you have other trousers?" she asked him pointedly.

"Of course I do," he said casually, setting his coffee on the windowsill and opening up the paper with a flourish.

Ivy sighed, the pretence at not understanding her hints were incredibly annoying. "Could you go put them on?"

Her father peered at her. "Ivy, there is nothing wrong with a man wearing his underwear in his own home. It's comfortable."

"But Dad!" Ivy whined. "I'm in your own home too!"

Robert looked away from her again and studied his paper. "I noticed."

Ivy sighed dramatically as her mother entered, looking significantly smarter than Ivy was used to seeing on a Sunday morning.

"Oh good," she said, smiling excitedly. "You're up."

"Yeah," said Ivy, sipping her coffee. "Sort of."

"Your father and I have decided it's time for you to stop moping."

"I'm not moping," she said. "I'm processing."

"Spending your days watching nonsense on TV and eating all my Doritos is moping."

"Eurgh," Ivy grunted, snuggling deeper into her blanket and looking away from her mother.

"Ah, there's my teenager again," said Ivy's mother, hands on her hips. "I thought we'd got through the days of monosyllabic grunting."

"I wish I WAS a teenager again," she said grumpily. "Maybe then I could do something to prevent my life from collapsing around me in a heap of despair and chaos."

"Probably not," said her father, not looking up.

Ivy glared at him. "You're not funny."

"I assume you're going to dye your hair purple and paint your room black again?" he asked.

"It wasn't black," said Ivy. "It was Desolation Raven."

"So, pretentious black," said her father, turning a page in his paper.

"The point is," said Emmeline, interrupting their snarking, "It's time to move on. I'm sick of this. We go to work, you're like this. We come home, you're like this, but with wine," her mother looked cross. "We didn't raise you to be this person."

"Maybe I like being this person," said Ivy, nestling down more deeply into her blanket.

"Nobody likes you being this person," said Emmeline, folding her arms. "There has been enough sadness, enough tears, and enough letting your life slip away because a stupid man couldn't appreciate you and respect you enough to let you flourish. You are not going to be defined by this one event, Ivy. I won't let my only daughter decompose into a swamp because of some knobhead man. You need to get some self-respect. Do you hear me?"

"Yes," grumbled Ivy. "I hear you."

"Your father and I are not made of money, Ivy, and right now I don't think you appreciate that. We are happy to support you. We've always been happy to support you. But you're a grown woman and you need to start acting like it!"

"Jeez, Mum. Fine! I get it! I'll start sorting my life out!"

"Well, I hope you do," said Emmeline with a sharp nod. "Now go upstairs and get dressed. Nicely."

Ivy looked at her mother suspiciously. The pep talk was one thing, the command to dress nicely was another, "Why?" she asked, suspiciously.

"Your father's friend, Malcolm, is coming by in a bit."

"So?" asked Ivy.

"So, he's got a job opening."

"I thought you wanted me to go back to school," said Ivy, petulantly.

"I did," she said. "But you're not."

"You're lounging around, rotting in your own bacteria," said her father.

"You know, you don't have to contribute to these conversations if you don't want to," Ivy said to him.

"Go and get showered and dressed," said her mother. "Wash your hair. And put on something that isn't made of Lycra or fluff."

Ivy moaned and heaved herself up. "Fiiiiiiiiiiiine."

"Good girl," she said.

"Make sure Dad puts his trousers on," said Ivy as she stomped upstairs.

Upstairs, she showered, blow-dried her hair, and dressed in the smartest thing she could be bothered to dig out - a pair of jeans and the only long-sleeved t-shirt in the pile that didn't have ketchup down the front. Not her usual job interview style by any stretch, but if her mother expected something more impressive then she should have given her more notice.

Heading back downstairs, Ivy heard voices in the kitchen and braced herself. She was *so* not in the mood for this, but apparently the emotional outpouring last night had awakened a desire in her mother to move on from the shitshow of Ivy's marriage, and if she knew anything about her mother, it was that she was incredibly motivated in anything she decided to do.

Ivy took a moment to breathe deeply and find some sense of inner calm before she stepped into the kitchen. Feeling very self-conscious and realising this was the first time she had actually been expected to behave like an adult in a very long time, she saw her parents drinking coffee at the kitchen table with a man she presumed was Malcolm.

Her mother stood up, arms wide, as she greeted her enthusiastically.

"Ivy!" she sang out.

Ivy stood awkwardly in the doorway and waved a hand. "Hello," she said.

"Come, sit down," said her mother, gesticulating theatrically towards the empty chair.

Ivy approached the table, feeling their eyes following her. She felt like she was a prize cow being offered up for sale.

"Ivy," said her father, rather formally. "This is Malcolm. You met him once before, do you remember?"

Malcolm stood and held out his hand. "Lovely to see you, Ivy." He said, a smile in his eyes.

Ivy shook it politely. "No, I don't remember, sorry," she said, returning the smile. "But it's nice to meet you."

"You do!" insisted her mother. "Malcolm Cope!"

"I don't remember, sorry," said Ivy again.

"He has a daughter."

"Well, that certainly narrows it down, thank you, Mother," said Ivy, going to the coffee pot and getting more caffeine as they all sat back down.

"Her name is... erm..." started Emmeline. Ivy turned and smiled at her mother, amused, as she struggled to recall the fabled daughter's name.

"Seren," said Malcolm, gently reminding her, no note of judgment in his voice for Emmeline forgetting.

"What a lovely name!" gasped Emmeline as Ivy sat at the table with them and sipped her coffee.

"Because she's my star," said Malcolm, smiling warmly. Ivy realised she liked this man and she wanted him to like her. She didn't know much about him, admittedly, but if a job was on offer, he seemed like he'd be a significantly nicer person to work for than Hugh Bright. "She's only a couple of years older than you, Ivy. You played together a couple of times, if I remember correctly."

"Yes," said Ivy's father. "Before you and Laura moved to... Devon was it?"

"That's right. North Tawton. Laura's family had roots there and it had been her dream to live there," he said, before turning back to Ivy. "After Laura passed, I decided I'd move back here and start over. It didn't feel right to be living her dreams anymore. I decided it was time to have a go at living mine instead. I'd never really backed myself enough to do it but Laura inspired me. So, that's why I'm here."

"I'm so sorry for your loss," said Ivy. "Laura sounds like a lovely person."

For a moment Malcolm's eyes glazed but then he smiled. "She was. I truly believe she would be pleased to know her daft old goat of a husband had finally got around to doing what I always said I'd do. Only forty years late!"

Ivy smiled. "That's nice." Maybe, she mused, she'd finally become an architect in forty years' time. Seventy-year-old architects were a thing, surely?

"You met her too of course, but I'm not surprised you don't remember," he said. "You were about five at the time, if I remember rightly."

"Oh, well that explains it," said Ivy laughing.

"You told me your My Little Pony had farted on my shoe."

"Ah," said Ivy.

"She was quite precocious," said Emmeline.

"So, Ivy," said Malcolm, leaning in and looking seriously. "Your dad tells me you've recently been made redundant from a job in sales?"

"Yes," said Ivy. "Hot tubs."

"I see," said Malcolm nodding. "Well, I have to say I haven't got anything remotely similar available to offer you."

"Oh, that's fine!" Ivy insisted. "I'm not a dedicated hot tub salesperson. I hated it to be honest. I only worked there because I needed a job and they were willing to hire me."

"Our Ivy was going to be an architect," said Robert.

"'Til she married that swine," said Emmeline darkly.

"Mum!" Ivy hissed.

As interviews went, this was definitely one of the most awkward. Though not the worst. That would be the manager for the spa resort that casually mentioned that working in a bikini was encouraged. Or the bar manager who touched her thigh as they were talking before giving her a meaningful look.

"Sorry, darling," said her mother, holding her hands up. "Not the time. Do go on."

Ivy took a moment then turned to Malcolm, her best job interview smile on her face and straightening out her T-shirt. "I was going to do my Masters, but I have an almost-completed degree in Design Engineering and several years of experience in a variety of office-based jobs."

"Excellent," said Malcolm, nodding. "That sounds great, Ivy."

Ivy's parents looked incredibly pleased. Ivy recognised those faces from the days of Parents' Evenings. The regression of moving back home was clearly impacting them all.

"Thanks," said Ivy, nodding.

"Well, I am confident that you'd fit in very well with us, and I'd like to offer you the position," said Malcolm. "If you'd like it?"

Ivy hesitated. She suddenly realised she had no idea what she was actually signing up to. Her parents had told her nothing. All she knew about this man was that he loves his daughter and had experience in handling unicorn fart.

"I'm sorry," she said, awkwardly. "I don't actually know what the position is."

"Oh!" said Malcolm with an apologetic laugh. "I own a theme restaurant. We need a greeter."

Ivy chewed her lip. "What's the theme?"

Chapter Ten

"Welcome to The Seven Seas Restaurant," said Ivy to a family of six, her practised smile firmly on her face.

The children all gawped, and Ivy understood why. The theme of the restaurant was somewhere between 'Under the Sea' and 'Pirates of the Caribbean', inspired by Malcolm's time on the coast of Devon. There were nets with plastic lobsters in hung from the ceiling, huge fish adorning every wall, and a light display that made the ceiling look like it was rippling water. All the floor staff wore fancy dress, and there was an enormous blue whale statue dominating the middle of the restaurant.

Ivy liked to refer to it as subtle.

"Look, Mummy," whispered the smallest of the children, pulling at her mother's cardigan. "A mermaid!"

Ivy smiled down at the child and tossed the long green hair of her wig over her shoulder. She crouched down and whispered. "I'm not a mermaid, look I've got legs!"

"What are you then?" asked the girl, looking crestfallen, examining Ivy's shiny green, scale pattern leggings with suspicion.

"I'm a water nymph," said Ivy, giving her a knowing look. "I can swim under water like a mermaid AND walk on land like a person. I've got a pet turtle, I ride a dolphin like a horse, and I can speak whale."

"Wow," whispered the girl, her eyes wide. "That's so cool!"

Ivy grinned at her and stood up. The little girl's mother looked at her with a broad smile. "Thank you, Mabel's been so excited to come!"

"You're absolutely welcome," said Ivy. "Do you have a reservation?"

"Goldstein for six," said the mother.

Ivy checked her screen them smiled at them. "Right this way."

Ivy turned and headed through the restaurant, the family keeping in line behind her. All the way she could hear Mabel gasping excitedly as she pointed out different décor and clapping her hands with joy. The oldest of the siblings seemed decidedly unimpressed and was getting a quiet scolding from his father.

"Here you go," said Ivy as they got to their table. The family all took seats, the children squabbling over who got to sit next to the octopus, as Ivy turned to see Ben Cope, dressed like a knock-off Jack Sparrow, approaching with a grin on his face. "Your waiter today is Captain Ben. He'll take care of you from here."

"Bye!" whispered Mabel.

Ivy gave her a wave then headed back to her podium, hearing Ben greet them with an enthusiastic and theatrical, "Argh! Whadda we have here then?"

She smiled to herself as she walked, then her face fell as she saw Mya and Julia waiting at the podium, looking far too delighted to see her. Ivy flipped her long green hair behind her shoulders and strode towards them.

"Good Lord above," Ivy groaned. "What are you doing here?"

"I'm pretty sure that's not the official greeting," said Mya, hands on her hips and a goofy smile on her face.

"Mya Shaw, you are tripping if you think I'm giving you the full spiel."

"Well... it's not unheard of," said Mya shrugging.

"We've been dying to get a look at your costume!" squealed Julia with a childish delight.

Ivy sighed and laughed, then gave them a twirl, displaying her shiny fish scale leggings, seashell decorated top, and bum-length green wig.

"I'm impressed they've not gone full Hooters," said Mya, nodding her approval. "When you said nymph, I was imagining..." Mya pushed her boobs together and pouted.

"Yeah," said Ivy, remembering her relief when Malcolm had shown her the outfit. "Luckily it's just a bit embarrassing, not exploitative."

"I think you look adorable," said Julia. "It really suits you."

"To be fair, it's making me tempted to go green," agreed Mya, scruffing up her pink pixie cut. "Of course, I could've done a better effect on your face."

Mya peered at Ivy's make-up and sparkly decorations around her eyes, hastily applied in the cloakroom at the back of the restaurant each morning. Mya, an expert in theatrical and cinematic make-up and special effects make-up, would have no doubt created something with silicone and layers of paint that made Ivy look incredible.

"Yes," agreed Ivy. "But I did this without six hours in the make-up chair."

Mya shrugged. "We all have our priorities."

"We don't have time for a meal, we've both got work to get back to," said Julia. "We just wanted to see you."

"Is there a bar?" asked Mya. "Or is it all... fish."

"There's a bar, I'll put you down for two seats," said Ivy, tapping on the computer screen.

"When do you get a break?" Julia asked her.

"Soon," said Ivy, checking the time. "I'll get one of the waitresses to come and cover me and I'll come join you soon. The bar's just past that whale."

Julia and Mya headed off for drinks as another family with excited children came in.

"Welcome to The Seven Seas Restaurant!" said Ivy, reapplying her smile.

When Ivy got a chance, she gestured for Daisy - who was dressed, unfortunately, as a lobster - to cover her podium, then she slipped away to the bar, waving at excited children as she went past.

Mya and Julia were perched on stools at the bar, drinking cocktails and chatting.

"How's it going?" Ivy asked, as she slipped into a bar chair on the other side of Julia. "I feel like I've not seen you in ages!"

"You haven't," said Julia, an eyebrow raised. "It's been, what...three weeks?"

"Nearly four," said Mya, pointedly.

"Nearly four weeks!" said Julia.

"Sorry," said Ivy.

"Fred's not impressed," said Julia "He was getting quite used to regular evenings alone with greasy take-out food and films where men beat the crap out of each other for inexplicable reasons."

"Well," said Ivy, laughing. "Please pass on my apologies to Fred. I think my mother is grieving them too; we've got a back log of junk food and wine."

"Tell her to throw it my way," said Mya. "I'm always available to help!"

"I'll let her know," said Ivy, laughing.

"So, it's going well?" Mya asked.

"Yeah," said Ivy, shrugging. "I mean it's going, you know? It's not like the job I always wanted or anything, but I like it a lot more than the last one. More standing up, which my feet aren't quite adjusted to yet, and keeping this ridiculous outfit clean is quite a hassle, but it's fun. It's nice to see how happy the kids are and the people who work here are dead nice."

"That's good," said Julia, smiling. "It's good to see you starting to... you know..."

"Live?" asked Ivy.

"Yeah," said Julia. "Live."

"Sorry I've been such a Moaning Myrtle," said Ivy, looking sheepish. "I kinda lost my shit a bit there."

"A bit?" asked Mya. "Ivy, you were a ruin."

"Not that we're judging you for it!" said Julia, looking at Mya sternly. "It's just good to see you doing... erm... better."

"Thanks guys," she said. "Genuinely."

"So, what's the money like?" asked Mya, sipping her cocktail and looking innocent.

"Mya!" said Julia, aghast. Julia appreciated rules and traditional manners. Mya did not.

"What? I've never dressed like a fish for work," said Mya, shrugging.

"I'm not a fish, I'm a water nymph," said Ivy, holding a leg up. "See? No tail."

"My mistake," said Mya, nodding sagely.

"The money's okay," said Ivy, shrugging. "It's less than I was on before, but Mum's not charging me rent yet, so it doesn't really matter that much. I'm basically a kid with a paper route."

"And how's that going?" asked Julia. "Living at home again."

Ivy sighed and rubbed her eyes. "Fine, I guess," she said. "I mean I don't want to complain. I had to give up the house; there was no real choice. The rent was affordable for a doctor... not a fish."

"Water nymph," corrected Mya.

"And I'm dead grateful you know?" she went on. "I bring home groceries and stuff to help out, but they always refuse to take actual money. And it means I'm starting to save a little, which could come in super helpful when I do get my own place again."

"But?" asked Julia, apparently sensing the hesitation in Ivy's voice.

"But... I feel a bit pathetic, to be honest. I haven't been this dependent on my parents since I was a teenager. I'm sleeping in a single bed; my mum treats me like I'm a child, and my dad leaves his toenail clippings on the coffee table."

"Oh, good lord," gasped Julia, and took a sip of her cocktail.

"Plus, it's on the wrong side of town for work. I'm trying to avoid using my car to save money, but the buses are rubbish, and it's just..." Ivy sighed. "It's just frustrating."

"Do you want to come and stay with me for a bit?" asked Julia.

Ivy looked at her, surprised. "Really?"

"We've got a spare room," said Julia, shrugging. "It's yours if you want it."

"But... Fred?"

"Oh, he won't mind," said Julia. "You know Fred."

"Are you sure?"

Julia shrugged. "He'll get over it."

"It wouldn't be forever."

"I know," said Julia.

"And I'll help out, with money and food and stuff," Ivy felt herself panic-rambling. "And I'm a good house guest I promise. I'll clean up and I'll cook, I mean not as well as you cook because I can't really cook anything fancy, and you have all those French recipe books and jars of herbs I can't pronounce, but I do make a good omelette and..."

"It's fine, Ivy," said Julia, putting a hand on hers.

Ivy chewed her lip. It was seriously tempting. Her mother might be upset that she was leaving, but her father would probably throw a celebration by walking around in just pants and socks, scattering toenail clippings like confetti, and tooting a trumpet without anybody complaining about it.

"It's just around the corner," said Mya. "You'd be daft not to do it."

Ivy eyed Julia nervously, looking for any trace of doubt, but Julia seemed calm and open about the whole thing.

"Stop scrutinising my face," said Julia. "I wouldn't offer if I didn't mean it. So, what do you say?"

"Yes," said Ivy, nodding gratefully. "I would really appreciate that. Thanks, Julia."

Mya and Julia clinked cocktail glasses.

"Gah! Avast ye maties!" came a voice from behind her. Ivy looked round to see Ben approaching, fully committing to the pirate role with a drunken swagger.

"Hi Ben," she said, rolling her eyes at him with a laugh.

"Hello there, me hearties," he greeted, sweeping off his hat and bowing to them.

"Ben, these are my friends, Mya and Julia," said Ivy.

"That be rum you're drinking?" he asked them, peering at their glasses.

"This is Ben Cope," said Ivy. "He's the boss. And he enjoys this far too much."

Ben held out his hand to Mya and Julia, and they both shook it.

"Nice to meet you fine ladies," he said with a grin, dropping the pirate act.

"I thought Malcolm was the boss?" asked Mya, looking Ben up and down.

"Technically I'm more of a boss in training." Said Ben. "Malcolm Cope is my uncle."

"Nice to meet you," said Julia, giving Ben a similar examination to Mya before flashing a look towards Ivy.

"So, boss's nephew," said Mya, leaning back. "You couldn't nepotise your way into a job that doesn't require a costume?"

Ivy kicked Mya under the bar, but Ben just laughed. "Normally I'm not out front," he said. "I nepotised my way into following Uncle Mal in management. He's training me up."

"So how come you're... this?" asked Julia.

"Uncle Mal believes managers should understand the work from the ground up," said Ben. "So, when someone's away, we cover their shifts. Everything from the cleaners to the cooks. We learn it all. The Cap'n is in Majorca, so, here I am!"

"Well, it suits you," said Mya, eyeing Ivy.

"Cheers," said Ben. "And like Ivy says, I do have a lot of fun with it." Ben suddenly went into pirate mode again. "But, me hearties, anything is more fun than spreadsheets."

They laughed appreciatively, and he slipped behind the bar to get a glass of water. Mya and Julia stared at Ivy.

"What?" Ivy whispered.

Mya and Julia gave each other a look as Ben came back out from behind the bar and back over to them. "Right," he said, smiling warmly. "I'll see you in a bit, Ivy. It was nice to meet you, Mya, Julia."

Ben gave a friendly wave and headed back off with his jaunty swagger as Mya and Julia turned back to Ivy.

"What?" Ivy asked again, but out loud this time.

"He is all kinds of delicious," said Mya, nodding in Ben's direction where he was performing for a group of children who were squealing in delight.

"What's your point?" asked Ivy, sitting upright awkwardly.

"I think what she's suggesting," said Julia. "Is that... you know... well... you should..."

"Lick him," said Mya, far too loudly. "Or better yet, get him to lick you."

"Jesus Christ, guys!" cried Ivy, looking around nervously. "He's my boss!"

"Just a suggestion," said Mya, eyeing Ivy as she sipped her cocktail.

"For the record," said Julia. "I was thinking you could go out for a drink with him. No licking involved."

"No licking involved!?" asked Mya incredulously. "This is what getting married does to the brain."

"Well... no licking, for NOW," said Julia, elbowing Mya.

"Guys," said Ivy, holding up her hands. "You have to stop."

"Why?" asked Mya. "He's hot, you're hot - what's the problem? Is he married?"

"No," said Ivy. "I mean, maybe, I don't know."

"You know," said Julia, smiling, far too amused for Ivy's liking.

"Yes, I know!" said Ivy, exasperated. "But not because I intended to find out. Daisy, Malia and Gary all fancy the arse off him and I overheard their conversation."

"Oh sure," said Mya, nodding to Julia. "She 'overheard'."

"Not listening in," agreed Julia.

"Definitely not," said Mya, nodding.

"Come on guys," sighed Ivy. "It's not about whether he's hot. He's OBVIOUSLY hot. The point is, I'm not ready for anything like that regardless of who it's with. I just need... time. More of it. Much more."

"Okay," said Julia, nodding. "We're sorry, Ivy."

"It's okay," said Ivy. "So, I'll be round after I've picked up some stuff from my mum's, is that okay?"

"Absolutely," said Julia.

Ivy slipped off her chair and straightened out her wig. "I can trust you to make Mya behave?"

Mya snorted. Julia put a hand on her arm. "You can count on me."

Chapter Eleven

Like everything else about Julia, her home was significantly more grown-up and elegant than anything about Ivy. It was like the posh spa hotel Ivy's mum had taken her to where everything was glistening and breakable, and the air carried the scent of expensive perfume. Yet, Julia had always been very relaxed about having Ivy and her clumsiness, and Mya and her... well... Myaness, in her house.

Dragging her suitcase from her car to the front door, that was surrounded by neatly maintained roses like something from a picture book, Ivy rang the doorbell, feeling oddly hesitant. She'd not lived with a friend since university, and she'd never lived with Julia. What if Julia could only cope with small doses of her? What if, a week in, she was paying someone to waft sage around and changing the locks?

For a moment, Ivy considered running back to the car with her bag and reclaiming her bed in her mother's house, but before she got a chance to, Julia had swung the door open with a broad smile.

"Welcome!" she said, enthusiastically.

Ivy dragged her suitcase into the house, where Julia pushed a glass of red wine into her hand as Fred appeared and took her suitcase from her.

"Thanks again, guys," said Ivy, once inside the impeccably tasteful living room. Amongst the shades of grey and soft silver, Ivy's bright green leggings and shell-decorated top made her stand out like a zit on a super model.

"You're welcome," said Julia, smiling. "She's welcome, isn't she, Fred?"

"You're welcome," agreed Fred. "Should I take this up for you?"

"Is that okay?" asked Ivy.

"Sure, no problem," said Fred, hoisting it up and heading upstairs.

"Thanks!" Ivy called after him.

"Is that everything?" asked Julia, leading Ivy into the kitchen, where amazing smells were wafting from a pan on the stove.

"No," said Ivy, slipping onto a stool at the kitchen island and picking up one of the sundried tomatoes Julia had put out on a platter of nibbles. "The rest is still back at mum's and dad's. I just brought the essentials really."

Fred came back down the stairs, sweating slightly. "That's a lot of essentials."

Julia glared at him then smiled back at Ivy. "You're welcome for a long as you need."

"It won't be for long," she said. "I just need to find a new place."

"How many have you looked at?" asked Fred.

"Well," said Ivy, awkward. "None, yet..."

"Oh, right," said Fred, forced nonchalance oozing out of him. "But you've been checking around, yeah?"

"Well... I..." No, she hadn't. She'd been putting it off. Somewhere in the back of her mind she was still clinging to the idea that Steven would realise the error of his ways and come running back, like everyone had said he'd do weeks ago. But she hadn't heard from him, hadn't seen him. Logically, she knew that it was over and it was time to move on, but still... if she made the commitment of getting a new home sorted, she was officially saying goodbye to the home she'd had. Not the house they'd lived in, but the home with Steven. So, no, she hadn't checked around. Not even once.

"I, erm..." Ivy stuttered.

When they'd first moved into that house, they'd been so excited. It had been decorated so badly and needed completely redoing, but Steven had been able to use the condition of it to get the rent reduced and it was much bigger than they'd have been able to afford otherwise.

They'd sat on the floor in the living room, eating Chinese take away straight from the tubs, off the top of a closed cardboard box full of books, and how they'd laughed with joy. They'd imagined turning the shambles into their beautiful home and spent the evening eating, drinking and flirting with one another.

Then, slightly drunk and full of food, they'd headed to bed, made love and held one another, dreaming of the years they'd spend there and the memories they'd infuse into the bricks with their laughter and love.

That box of books had served as their coffee table for weeks, until one day Steven had come home with a beautiful glass-topped piece that he'd bought from an antique shop as a surprise for her. That night they'd sat on the floor and eaten Chinese take-away straight from the tubs again, but from the top of the new coffee table, the box of books now opened in the corner and half unpacked onto the shelves.

She hadn't looked for somewhere new. She *couldn't* look for somewhere new.

Ivy blinked at Fred, the memories and the emotions threatening to overwhelm her. He sighed and nodded. "It's alright," he said. "I'm sure you'll be ready soon."

"Come on," said Julia, linking an arm through Ivy's. "Let me show you your room and how to jiggle the handle."

Ivy nodded. "Thanks, Julia," she said, smiling gratefully.

As they walked past Fred, Julia whacked him on the arm. Fred mouthed "What?" at her, holding up his arms in protest but Julia ignored him and headed up the stairs with Ivy.

The spare room was as elegant as the rest of the house. Plain white sheets, soft cream walls, and some fancy artwork that looked like it cost more than Ivy made in a year.

"Wow," breathed Ivy, sitting on the bed. The quilt felt like it had been woven together by sleep angels. She bounced lightly. "This is... swanky."

Julia shrugged. "Two good incomes, no kids." She sat down next to Ivy. "Are you okay?"

"I guess," said Ivy. No, she wasn't okay, but she was holding it together and for now that was enough.

"Have you heard from him?" asked Julia.

"Since he rendered me homeless?"

"Yeah," said Julia, gently.

"Nope," said Ivy, playing casual about as well as Fred played nonchalant.

"You still don't know where he is?"

"Nope."

"Crazy," said Julia, shaking her head. Crazy was one word for it. Ivy had loads of others. "Listen, I'll go get dinner on. Take your time and settle in, come down when you're ready, yeah?"

"Thanks," said Ivy.

"It'll be okay, Ivy," she said, standing up. "I promise."

Ivy nodded and forced a smile onto her face. When Julia stepped out of the bedroom and closed the door with a soft click, Ivy let tears pour down her face.

It'll be okay. But it'll be okay without Steven. And is that ever really going to be okay?

***

Dinner was delicious. Fred didn't mention finding somewhere else to live again. They ate the incredible risotto that had been releasing such delicious aromas, they drank more red wine, and they chatted while gentle classical music lilted away in the background. It was nice.

It was calmer than at her parents', though her mother had texted her about seventy-three times to make sure she was settled in okay and to profess her love and how much Ivy was missed. Her father had texted her once, to ask her where she'd left the remote control.

When Ivy went to bed, she didn't cry. She lay down, nuzzled into her ridiculously comfortable pillow, and fell asleep, the soft scent of fresh lavender coming from somewhere inexplicable.

The next day she was able to walk to work, and, having not sussed out the time difference, she arrived twenty minutes early.

Ben, only half-pirated, was sipping a cup of coffee at the bar. "Hey," he waved her over. "You're early."

"Well, I'm just that dedicated to the job," said Ivy, shrugging as she approached him.

"Sure," he said, giving her a half smile. "Why really?"

"I moved in with my friend, Julia," she said. "You met her a couple of weeks ago."

"Yeah, I remember," he said, smiling.

"She only lives round the corner," Ivy explained. "I haven't quite adjusted to being so close."

"Do you want a coffee? Most people won't be here for at least ten more minutes."

"Yeah, that'd be great." She went to head around the bar to the coffee machine, but Ben held up a hand and got up.

"Let me," he said.

"Oh, thanks."

Ivy awkwardly sat on a bar stool, a couple down from the one Ben had been occupying, watching him as he worked. He smiled round at her, and, feeling her cheeks burn, Ivy quickly looked down at her fingers. Mya would be making a right face at her if she caught Ivy leering. She busied herself getting her wig out of her bag and carefully brushing it.

Ben looked over his shoulder and smiled at her again. She carefully didn't look up, brushing the wig out and acting as oblivious as she possibly could.

"So," he said, setting a coffee in front of her and leaning on the bar with a dishcloth over his shoulder, like someone from an American diner in an old movie. "How are you settling in here?"

Ivy carefully set the wig down on the chair next to her before taking the coffee in her hands. She sipped it. It was perfect. Exactly how she liked it.

"Good," she said. "I like it here."

"Bit different from office life," he said. "Uncle Mal says you came from sales."

"Well, I've done a bit of everything," said Ivy, shrugging. "Never in shiny scales and a wig before, of course."

"Wish I could say the same," said Ben.

Ivy raised her eyebrows and laughed. Ben grinned and headed back out from behind the bar to the seat down from Ivy's.

"Well, I'll be back in civvy clothes next week," he said. "Jordan gets back at the weekend."

"Ah, okay," said Ivy, pretending she wasn't disappointed. "Jordan's nice."

"Yeah, good man," said Ben, nodding.

They sat quietly drinking their coffees for a moment.

"Well, it's been good while it lasted," said Ivy, smiling. Then kicked herself. Was she flirting? *Don't flirt. Fuck's sake. Don't flirt.*

"Yeah," said Ben, smiling at her. "The company down here is better than up there. The office crowd aren't quite as... scaly. Hopefully someone else will go on holiday soon."

Was he flirting? Was that even allowed? Was he looking at her? She stared at her coffee. *Don't make eye contact.* No, he wasn't flirting, that was wishful thinking. No not wishful thinking, crazy thinking. Not wishful. Definitely not wishful. *Oh bollocks.*

"Well," said Ivy, standing up and downing the last of her coffee so fast that she burned her throat and then coughed so much it sounded like a horse dying.

"Jesus, you okay?" asked Ben, standing up and coming to her side as she retched desperately.

"Yep!" she croaked, flapping a hand at him and staggering away backwards. "Just going to... head back there... nymph myself up properly!"

She grabbed her wig and waved it in the air maniacally before scurrying away to the locker room. *Get a bloody grip, Ivy Rhodes.*

***

"Good day?" asked Fred as Ivy came in that evening. He was perched on a stool at the kitchen island, tapping away on his iPad with a football match on the TV.

The air smelled of tomatoes, garlic and chilli and Ivy could see a pan of sauce simmering away on the stove. Living at Julia's was certainly working out well for her diet. She'd never eaten so well in her life. Her mother loved to cook, and her food was excellent, but Fred and Julia's skills were on another level. She wondered if they'd had private classes from Nigella.

"Yeah, not bad at all," she said. "Except I've just walked past a whole crowd of teenage boys who seemed quite fixated on asking me how mermaids have sex. And one asked to see my blow hole."

"What did he think you are?" asked Fred, laughing.

Ivy shrugged. "Who knows," she said. "Luckily, I'm only ten minutes' walk away now, so much less public humiliation than normal."

"Good," he said, smiling. "I've got spaghetti sauce on the hob and Julia should be home soon. She was held up by some meeting with the execs. Do you want a glass of wine?"

"In a min," said Ivy. "I'll go up and take a quick shower, wash the fish smell out of my hair, and be down in a bit."

"Cool, see you in a bit," said Fred, smiling at her then going back to his football.

When Ivy had washed and dressed in pyjamas, she found Julia downstairs with a glass of Shiraz, heels kicked off against the wall, and tasting Fred's sauce, her husband at her side.

"This is why I married you," she said, sighing happily then kissing him tenderly.

Ivy slipped into a chair at the island to join them. Fred slipped an arm around Julia and rested his cheek against her head. She felt like she was intruding on something so private and so intimate. They looked so at peace. So contented. She didn't know if she should announce herself with a timely cough or slip away and give them their privacy.

As she watched them stirring the sauce and sipping their wine, she felt her mind start to wander.

She and Steven had been contented. Cooking together was so rare; his long hours and changing shift patterns usually left the meals to be her responsibility, but he'd always enjoyed her efforts. Sometimes she'd wake up at midnight, hearing him come home and go rooting around for whatever meal she'd left covered up in the microwave for him. She'd get out of bed and come through, to find him still in hospital scrubs, hunched over the kitchen table eating warmed up lasagne, or chilli, or cottage pie, gratefully shovelling it in. She'd slip her arms around his waist and rest her cheek against the spot on his back between his shoulder blades, listening to his enthusiastic eating, and feeling his tired, warm body against her own.

She felt emotion start to flood her again and sniffed fruitily.

"Oh, hi!" Julia said as she turned around, startled by the sound, and spotted Ivy sitting there. "Good day?"

"Yeah," said Ivy, pushing thoughts and feelings about Steven as far down as she could stomach. "Not bad at all."

"Excellent," said Julia, leaving Fred cooking and fetching another glass from the cupboard.

"How about you?" asked Ivy as Julia sat in a seat next to her and poured wine into the glass.

"Really good actually," said Julia. She handed the second glass to Ivy and held her own up. "It's good to have you here, Ivy."

"It's good to be here," said Ivy, and they clinked glasses.

Ivy sipped her wine and pretended it was the truth. But it wasn't. The painful truth she was trying to ignore was that she would rather be with Steven.

Chapter Twelve

Ivy had been living with Julia and Fred for a month and had learned the timing for her walk to The Seven Seas Restaurant perfectly now. She was able to arrive with exactly the right amount of time to get clocked in, her make-up done, and her wig on so she could get to her podium with moments to spare.

"Early again," said Ben, looking up as Ivy came in one Thursday morning.

He was perched at the end of the bar, drinking coffee and going through some paperwork, as she was used to seeing him now, dressed smartly in tan trousers and an open-necked black shirt, with the sleeves rolled up to reveal a tattoo of a jigsaw puzzle piece on his forearm.

"Fancied a walk," said Ivy, shrugging as she walked towards the bar.

"Coffee?" he offered.

"Thanks, but I really don't mind making it," she insisted as she put her bag on the bar stool.

"I know," he said, getting up. "But you'd be doing me a favour. I need a break from these numbers."

"Thanks," said Ivy, sitting on a seat a couple down from where Ben had set up his workstation.

"Things not going well at your mate's?" asked Ben as he busied himself with the coffee machine.

"Why?" asked Ivy.

"You seem to be fancying a walk before your shift starts quite often," he said. "I wondered if you're just looking for an excuse to get out of there."

Ivy blushed and started to sweat. *Dammit.* "Nooo," she said, shaking her head. "Not at all! It's great. Julia's awesome. It's fab!"

Fab. She hadn't said 'fab' since she was fifteen. And she knew her voice was too high pitched. She sounded fifteen too. *Come on, Ivy, stop being ridiculous!*

He brought the coffee over and settled himself back down. "That's good," he said.

Ivy was about to speak when she heard the doors opening behind them. She turned and saw Daisy coming towards them looking annoyed but like she was pretending not to be.

"Oh! Ivy!" she said. "I wasn't expecting to see you here."

Oh god. Oh god, oh god, oh god.

Daisy stood between Ivy and Ben, a broad smile on her face and, Ivy noticed, more lipstick than was frankly necessary when she spent the day dressed as a lobster.

"Another early bird," said Ben.

"I guess we're just both... keen," said Daisy, raising her eyebrows at Ivy.

"A good quality in an employee!" said Ben, smiling and standing up. "You guys have some coffee; I'll head back there and give you some peace."

"Oh!" Daisy sounded devastated. "I didn't mean to chase you away!"

Ben gathered the papers into his laptop bag and put his computer under his arm.

"Not at all," he said. "I'll see you later."

"Okay, bye!" said Daisy, with a hint of desperation that irritated Ivy.

Ben gave them a friendly nod, then headed to the office at the back as Daisy turned to Ivy.

"So," she said, folding her arms and looking at her pointedly. "You're into Ben."

"I'm married!" Ivy protested.

"Aren't you divorced?"

"We've only been separated a few months," said Ivy.

"You're not into Ben?"

"Not at all," insisted Ivy. "I was just having a coffee before work and he happened to be here."

"Okay," said Daisy as she went round the bar to the coffee machine. "Good to know."

"Are... you... into him?" Ivy asked with as much nonchalance as she could muster.

"Darling," said Daisy pushing a cup under the spout. "We are ALL into him."

"Oh," said Ivy. Of course they were. Why wouldn't they be? I mean that was fine. It made no difference to her, since she was absolutely not even slightly ready to consider moving on from Steven. And even if she HAD been ready to move on from Steven, she was much too sensible to hit on her boss. She wouldn't even know HOW to hit on him. She wasn't sure if she'd ever hit on anybody ever.

And even if she had found herself feeling that way inclined, which she didn't, he clearly had a plethora of women just lining right up for the opportunity. Not that it mattered. Obviously.

"Right, I'm going to go get lobstered up," said Daisy, sighing. "Fuck me, I hate this job. Can you believe I did three years at LAMDA for this shit?"

Ivy laughed politely as Daisy stomped off, then finished her coffee alone, wondering whether Ben was into Daisy, and whether it even mattered if he was.

***

Later that evening, Ivy met Mya at Verso. Julia had gone to the theatre with Fred, so Mya had suggested a night out for them too.

Mya looked her usual brilliant self in a wrap-around cropped top and a necklace that looked like it was made from barbed wire and Ivy felt like a complete sack of potatoes next to her. They sat at the bar eating peanuts and drinking wine.

"Single life suits you," said Mya. "You look good."

"Sure," said Ivy.

"You do!" insisted Mya. "You look much less tense than I remember seeing you in ages."

"Well, thanks," said Ivy, shrugging. "I feel like shit, however."

"Ah love," said Mya. "It'll get better."

"Everyone keeps saying that," said Ivy. "But it doesn't seem to be happening."

"Give it time," said Mya.

"I guess," said Ivy. She took a sip of her wine and ate some more peanuts, but felt like she might want to order a pizza and cure her misery with cheese.

"Any movement with the hotty at work?" Mya asked.

"Who?" asked Ivy.

"Who?" Mya mimicked, rolling her eyes. "Like you don't know who I'm talking about, Ivy Rhodes."

"Ben?"

"No, the lobster woman," said Mya, rolling her eyes. "OBVIOUSLY Ben."

"No," said Ivy. "No movement."

"Booooo," said Mya. "You'd better get a move on. A man that fine won't be available forever."

Ivy shrugged. "He wouldn't be available at all if the lobster woman had her way."

"Trust me, you could take on the crustacean."

Ivy smiled. "Thanks, but I'm not going to try."

"Fine," said Mya with an overly dramatic sigh, then she brightened up. "I got some pretty good news."

"Yeah?"

"Amazing new job opportunity," she said, looking excited. "New Netflix show. Proper graphic violence, monsters, the works."

"That sounds amazing," said Ivy. "You'd be brilliant at that!"

"Definitely," said Mya. "I mean, I love my team, they're awesome, and the actors on this show actually aren't total knobs which makes a nice change. But anyone could do a slightly pink lip and some fluttery lashes. My skills are wasted there."

"Have you interviewed yet?"

"Yeah," said Mya. "Last week. The woman who interviewed me, Marilla, was brilliant. She's worked on some seriously high-end stuff. They've got access to some of the best kit in the world over there."

"When do you find out?"

"Soon," said Mya, crossing her fingers and closing her eyes for a moment.

"Well," said Ivy, holding up her glass. "Here's to your hopeful new job."

Mya smiled and held up her glass. They clinked and downed the rest of their wine.

"Hi there, two more please," said Mya to the woman behind the bar.

"Coming right up."

Mya turned back to Ivy as the woman started to refill their glasses. "And when are you going for a new job?" asked Mya. "You know, talking about being wasted."

Ivy sighed as she tapped her debit card on the card reader to pay for the wine. "I dunno," she said. "I've not really thought about it."

"Come on, Ivy!" cried Mya, putting her glass down heavily. "You're young, you're smart. Now you don't have Steven weighing you down like a bloody lead weight, you can go and be anything you want!"

"I guess," she said, picking at her thumbnail. "Just feels all a bit much, to be honest."

She knew logically she could go after what she wanted; she just didn't know what it was that she *did* want. All she'd ever wanted to be was an architect, and now she was a thirty-year-old water nymph. Without the potential of being an architect to aspire to, she felt lost. What other jobs were there? Everything interesting and good you had to train for, and she was too old to sink years into an education when she needed to live right now. She needed a new dream. Something attainable. Mya was right: she didn't dream of being a water nymph, but, equally, so she wasn't unhappy in the job, just unfulfilled.

"Well, you need to start getting a grip, in my opinion," said Mya. "And Julia's not here to make me behave, so I can say that to you. You're being a knob."

Ivy went to retaliate when she felt a hand on her shoulder. She spun around, surprised.

"Hello ladies," said the owner of the hand, which had thankfully been removed. A man, boy, who looked about twenty, with sandy blonde hair and a chin dimple, was standing uncomfortably close, with a friend at his side sipping a cocktail through a thin, pink straw.

"What do you want?" asked Ivy, tensing up and glaring at them.

"We couldn't help but notice you're sitting here all alone," said the other boy. A strong smell of Lynx was wafting from his Ben Sherman shirt.

"We're not alone," said Ivy, gesturing at Mya. "Clearly."

"He means," said the first man, "Without a gentleman to accompany you."

"This isn't fucking Gilead," said Ivy. "We're allowed out without male supervision, you know."

The two men exchanged confused looks. Mya snorted into her wine.

"Right, so, anyway," said the second man. "I'm Lee, and this is my brother, Lewis, and we'd like to buy you two ladies a round of drinks."

"We already have drinks," said Ivy, holding up her wine.

"More drinks..." said Lewis, a hint of desperation creeping into his voice.

Ivy sighed. "Save yourselves some time and money, boys, and give up now, yeah? I'm old enough to be your bloody mother for Christ's sake."

"We're actually celebrating her fiftieth birthday tonight," said Mya, nodding sagely.

Ivy shot them a cold smile.

Lewis elbowed Lee and nodded his head away from them. Lee sighed.

"Have a good night, ladies," said Lewis.

The two brothers headed away across the bar towards a group of women in the corner who were drinking some kind of lurid purple cocktail out of a fishbowl through straws.

"Well, you told them," said Mya.

Ivy shrugged. "I wasn't interested."

"Oh, I know," said Mya. "You made that very clear. But, maybe..."

"Maybe what?"

"Maybe it'd do you some good to have a little fun," she said. "Help you move on - you know - from him."

"Mya, they were practically teenagers."

"I don't mean you had to get your bloody leg over!" cried Mya. "I mean have a laugh. Have a flirt. Let them buy you a drink. You know, fun."

"No, thanks," said Ivy.

"You're not actually fifty you know, Ivy," Mya sighed.

Ivy shrugged and sipped her wine.

Mya watched her for a moment, a thoughtful look on her face, but Ivy chose to ignore it. She didn't want to get into it. She knew she had to move on, she knew one day she'd be ready to start trying for a new relationship, but not yet.

"So," said Ivy. "Tell me more about the new job. Who's the director?"

"Song Suzy. She's this awesome Korean woman," enthused Mya. "This is her first UK based gig."

"Yeah?"

"Yeah, she came from making these really amazing movies that are huge over there, and she takes no fucking shit," Mya laughed. "Like I met the DOP," Ivy looked blank, "Director Of Photography," Ivy nodded, "and he had some serious swagger on him, thought he was billy big boots, you know? She had none of it."

"Nice," said Ivy, nodding her approval. "Tell me everything."

They spent the rest of the evening talking about Mya's job, TV shows they'd been watching and books they'd been reading. Mya didn't mention Ben or Steven again, and the two brothers had found success with the cocktail women in the corner, so they didn't pester them either. When Ivy finally got home, she crept upstairs to bed to avoid waking Julia or Fred, and lay in bed, her mind racing.

Mya was so excited about her job. She'd worked hard, she'd done numerous courses to advance and qualify in special effects, art and make up, worked in apprenticeships and as a runner on film sets time and time again, and was now getting the work she'd always dreamed of. And she was happy. Julia had worked hard in university, got her degree, started in her firm as an assistant and was now making presentations to the execs. She was on track to become an executive herself before long. And she was happy.

What was Ivy? She wasn't happy, that was for sure.

***

Ivy stopped showing up early for work. She came at the right time, worked hard, and left again. She didn't seek out Ben's company, not because she didn't enjoy it, but because she wasn't sure why she enjoyed it and she wasn't ready to have that conversation with herself. She spent her evenings eating dinner with Julia and Fred, then curled up in the armchair while they sat together on the sofa, and they watched TV or films, sometimes just chatted. It was nice, it was comfortable. But it wasn't what she wanted.

One evening, after Fred and Julia had gone to bed, Ivy sat on her ridiculously comfy bed and turned on her laptop. Hesitantly, and without certainty that she was doing the right thing, she searched for architecture courses.

She started browsing through pages, looking at words she'd long forgotten, campuses full of happy young students, and she felt a pang in her heart. She wasn't ready for a new dream. There was only one dream she'd ever really wanted. She wanted that dream. But, how? She'd given up on the dream of becoming an architect for the dream of Steven, but then Steven had given up on her.

She closed the laptop again and pushed it to the bottom of the bed. Was it even possible? Can you be thirty, in a full-time job as a water nymph, and still go to university?

No. That was crazy.

She put the laptop on the desk and got under the duvet. It was time to move on with her life and let the past be in the past.

The idea didn't stop niggling at her mind though.

The next day, Malcolm Cope was walking across the restaurant when he spotted Ivy headed back to her podium after seating a happy little family and caught up to her.

"Ivy Rhodes," he greeted her, arms outstretched and a warm smile beaming across his kind face. "How's it going?"

Ivy glanced towards her podium, nobody was waiting so she stopped and gave him her full attention. She was always happy when Malcolm came onto the floor. "I'm fine, thanks" she said. "How are you?"

"Oh, very well," he said, smiling. "Enjoying seeing my little empire running so smoothly. I should make more time to mingle down here. I do love it so."

"I know you do," said Ivy smiling.

"It makes me very happy to see so many smiles," he said.

"Good," said Ivy. She was glad he was happy. He deserved to be happy.

"May I take a moment of your time, Ivy?"

"Erm," Ivy looked about, worried about leaving her podium unattended.

"Gary!" called out Malcolm, waving to Gary who was strolling past dressed like a jelly fish with shimmery plastic tendrils hanging around his head. "Can you pop over here for a moment?"

"Of course, Mr Cope," said Gary, trotting over and giving a little bob that was so close to a curtsy that Ivy cringed for the blushing jelly fish.

"Mind Ivy's podium for me for five minutes?"

"Of course, Mr Cope," said Gary again, managing to avoid the curtsy this time.

Malcolm gestured for Ivy to follow him to a quiet end of the restaurant where they sat at a table together. Ivy felt her heart banging. Her hands sweating. What had she done?

"Listen," he said quietly, leaning on his elbows and looking her in the eye. "Ben's been telling me that you're a brilliant worker, and certainly everyone has been impressed... but..."

Ivy panicked. But what? She couldn't be fired, could she!? Not again. Oh crap. She'd not done anything wrong!

"But?" asked Ivy. *Shit shit shit shit shit shit.*

"But he doesn't think you're happy here."

"What?"

"Are you happy here, Ivy?" he asked her, tilting his head to the side and examining her face in a slightly disconcerting way, as if he could read her mind. "Is this what you want?"

Ivy blinked. "Yes," she said after a moment. "I'm very happy here. Thank you."

"I see," he said, leaning back and folding his arms. He sat in silence for a moment, watching her thoughtfully. Ivy squirmed inside. "I know you were destined for things greater than my little restaurant. I wouldn't blame you for being dissatisfied."

"I don't believe in destiny," she said. "I believe in doing the best you can with what you get. And this is what I've got."

Malcolm smiled. "And you're definitely doing exceptionally well, by all reports."

"Thank you," said Ivy, sighing with relief.

Malcolm patted her arm. "I won't lie, I'm glad you're happy. It would be a shame to lose you."

"I'm not going anywhere," said Ivy.

"Excellent. Well, sorry for interrupting," he said. "Back to it then!"

He headed off to the office and Ivy returned to her podium, lots of thoughts wandering through her brain. Why did Ben think she wasn't happy? Was he hoping she'd leave? How often did he talk about her? How often did her feelings occur to him?

Was she really not going anywhere? Had she just accepted that this was her life now?

When Ivy got home, she found Fred and Julia cooking together in the kitchen, soft music playing, and a romantic atmosphere. Julia was resting her head on Fred's shoulder and his hand was in the back pocket of her jeans.

Ivy tried to slip past them, but Julia heard her and turned round, Fred's hand slipping out of her pocket as she did.

"Hi!" she said, looking happy to see her. "Good day?"

Behind her, Fred looked sadly towards his wife for a brief moment before he turned back to sauce-stirring without saying anything.

"Sure, fine," said Ivy. "I'll just head upstairs and give you guys some space."

"Stay!" insisted Julia. "Join us for a drink. Dinner will be ready soon. Spaghetti, with some roast chicken on the side for Fred."

"A man's gotta have his meat!" said Ivy.

"I'm not a caveman, Ivy," he said, turning to her and looking irritated. "I've been eating vegetarian for a while now and I just fancied some chicken."

"Oh!" Ivy flustered. "I wasn't meaning... I mean you don't have to... I was just joking I'm... I... It was a joke."

"Ignore him," said Julia quietly. "He's just feeling a bit grumpy."

"Sorry," said Ivy.

Julia shrugged and rubbed her arm. "I'll pour you a glass of wine."

Ivy glanced over at Fred, who was drinking and stirring the sauce, the romantic music playing as he stood alone.

"Okay," said Ivy. She was hungry and Julia was characteristically welcoming, but still, it didn't feel quite right. "I'll just go and put my stuff down upstairs."

"See you in a mo," said Julia, heading back into the kitchen.

When Ivy came back down, the music had been turned off and Julia was sitting at the island watching Fred as he finished the cooking. Ivy tentatively approached and Julia smiled at her and held up a glass of red wine.

"We okay?" Ivy asked, nervously, taking the glass of wine from Julia and slipping into one of the island seats.

"Of course," said Julia. "Aren't we, Fred?"

Fred turned to Ivy with a smile. "Absolutely," he said. "Sorry Ivy, I've had a long day."

Ivy nodded nervously. "No problem," she said.

Ivy sipped her wine and glanced at Fred as he kept his back to them and at Julia who was smiling broadly, her dark eyes glistening slightly. The silence was only broken when Fred turned around and announced the food was ready.

Chapter Thirteen

"Found your own place yet?" asked Ivy's mother before Ivy had even sat down at the table in Verso.

"No," said Ivy, lowering herself into the chair with a sigh. "Not yet, Mum."

As if her mother wouldn't know if Ivy had moved. The passive aggression wasn't amusing but she couldn't be bothered to call her out on it.

"Oh Ivy," said her mother. "Let me help! You know Henrietta at 96?"

"No?"

"Yes, you do!" insisted her mother.

"Let me stop you before we get into this dance, Mum," said Ivy with a tired sigh. "I don't know Henrietta, but pretend I do and just tell me why she's relevant."

Emmeline bristled slightly. "Fine. She works at Reeds Rains. I could ask her to keep an eye out for new listings in your price range."

"Thanks, but I don't think there's much available in my price range."

"There must be something!"

"Well, there probably is!" Ivy threw her hands up. "I don't know, alright? I'm not ready yet!"

Emmeline peered at her then handed her a menu. "Maybe you should move back home."

Ivy examined the menu, trying to ignore her mother. "No, thanks Mum."

"Ivy, it's not fair to Julia and Fred!"

"They're fine!" insisted Ivy, putting the menu down and looking around for a waitress. This was going to be one of those alcohol-requiring evenings, she could tell.

"They're a married couple," she said. "They need their space."

"You and Dad are a married couple," said Ivy.

"Yes, but we're old," she said. "Our days of swinging from chandeliers and shagging on the kitchen table are over. We couldn't get up there without breaking our necks or putting your father's back out again like last time."

Ivy screwed up her face. "Mum!"

"What?" she said. "You saw the mess he was in! Poor love could barely get off the toilet without help."

"I thought he'd done it clearing the bloody gutters, mother!" cried Ivy, exasperated, as she waved frantically at the waitress. "I told him he should get a man in to finish the job!"

Emmeline cracked up with laughter as the waitress approached. "Ready to order?"

"I'll have the tortellini," said Emmeline. "With a large chardonnay."

"The veggie pizza please," said Ivy. "And Pinot Grigio."

"Coming right up," said the waitress.

"Anyway," said Ivy. "Your and Dad's weird sex injuries aside, I'm close to work there, and Julia says I can stay as long as I want. And Fred always wears trousers in the living room."

"Ivy, darling," said her mother, leaning forwards. "In all seriousness. I think you need to move on with your life."

"Mum," said Ivy. "Please. Just let it go."

Her mother shrugged as the waitress came back with the drinks.

***

Ivy had Saturday night off, so was spending it curled in a chair reading a book, whilst Julia and Fred read the papers. Julia had put on some gentle jazz music, and they were eating olives and sun-dried tomatoes from a platter that Julia had laid out on the coffee table. It all felt very grown-up and civilised.

"Says here that property prices in the area are dropping," said Fred, straightening out the paper he was reading. Ivy looked up.

"Do you want to move?" asked Julia quizzically, as she plucked an olive from the dish.

"No," said Fred, casually. "Just an observation. I mean, say we WERE looking for a new home, now would be the ideal time to be looking."

Ivy shifted uncomfortably in her seat and pretended to put immense concentration into reading her book.

"What's your point?" asked Julia, her voice hardening.

"Nothing," said Fred, crossing his legs and leaning back, his display of nonchalance worthy of a BAFTA. "Oh, Ivy?!"

"Hmm?" Ivy looked up, feigning ignorance of the entire conversation.

"You've been looking around this area for a place to live," he said. "Have you noticed a change in property prices?"

Ivy blinked. Was it a trap? If she was emphatic that they had indeed dropped and he was bullshitting, she'd be busted. She had promised that she was looking at the estate agents' websites regularly, but just couldn't find anywhere affordable yet. But if she said no and he wasn't lying, she'd be exposed again. Julia and Fred were both looking at her.

Her back was sweating. Would Fred really be trapping her? Was he that sly?

"Ivy?" prompted Fred.

Oh god. Say something. Anything.

"I'm not great with numbers," she said after a moment. "I've not really noticed anything."

"Funny," said Fred, turning back to the article. "Because apparently it's affected both ends of the market. So really you should be noticing a lot more affordable properties in your price bracket."

"Drop it, Fred," said Julia.

Fred sighed. "I'm not being unreasonable here," he said. "You know you're always welcome here, Ivy, but if you ARE looking for a place, it's worth noting that now is a good time!"

"Yeah," said Ivy, standing up. "I... I think I'll go and have another look on my laptop now."

"Ivy!" said Julia. "You don't have to do that. It's fine! We're having a lovely evening here!"

"Let her go!" said Fred. "You know she needs to!"

"Needs to what?!"

"Move on! Get a life!"

Ivy felt herself recoil inwardly. This was horrific.

"She's still married!" cried Julia, standing up. "She doesn't have to rush herself to move on from that!"

"I'm not saying she has to rush!" said Fred, exasperated. "But at some point, she's going to need to grow up and stop living like a student! To do that she needs to embrace the inevitable!"

"She is taking her time and respecting her relationship!" protested Julia hotly.

Ivy backed away. "I'm, erm... headed up then..." she said quietly, but neither looked at her.

The silence that filled the room felt like aggressive electrical surges building to an impending explosion.

Ivy hurried up the stairs. As she reached the landing, she heard Julia break the silence. "Why are you being so pushy?!"

"Why aren't you?" asked Fred, equally exasperated.

"Because she's my friend!"

Ivy opened her bedroom door. She was going to go in but she stopped and listened. She knew she shouldn't. But she had to.

"I know she's your friend," came Fred's voice. "And it's not like I don't care about her too, you know I love Ivy to pieces! I've always loved her. But come on, Julia!"

"What?"

"This is getting ridiculous!" cried Fred. "She keeps saying she's looking for her own place but have you actually seen any evidence of that?!"

"I don't go checking up on her, Frederick!" Julia sounded angry. "And she's going through a hard time! I respect that she's not just quitting on her marriage, and so should you!"

"But she's invading ours!" Fred sounded angry now too. "I feel like we're not a couple anymore!"

Ivy felt her eyes burning and fought back tears, mostly because she didn't want to make a noise.

"Now you're being ridiculous!" said Julia, though her voice had lost some of its hostility.

"Am I? This is the first time we've been alone together in weeks!"

"We're alone together every night!" Julia sounded emotional and stressed. "It's not like she sleeps in our bed with us, is it!?"

"It bloody feels like it sometimes!" shouted Fred. "We don't even have sex anymore because you're worried Ivy will hear!"

"Shh!" hissed Julia.

"And now you're worried she'll hear us even mention it? You know what, Jules, maybe she needs to hear it! She has to know we can't live like this forever! It's like we're some weird sexless throuple!"

"Sex again!" raged Julia. "Is that the problem? You hoped that Ivy living here would result in some kind of fantasy threesome situation!"

"What?" cried Fred. "Are you mad? No!"

"Because that's what it sounds like to me! And trust me when I tell you I will walk out of this door if you even think I'll consider..."

"I said no!" shouted Fred. "Will you stop? Julia, come on!"

Julia was silent. Ivy assumed she was glaring at him with a challenge to explain himself. She'd seen Julia's stare of fury before and it had curdled milk.

"I'm serious, Julia," said Fred. "No, I do not want to initiate an incredibly awkward and tense three-way with your best friend. Because I'm not a porn-addled incel."

There was silence for a moment more, then Julia sighed. "Fine," she said, her voice softer. "So, what do you want?"

"I want it to be us again," said Fred. "That's all I want. Just us. I miss it. I miss... you."

There was quiet again, then Ivy heard movement as they came together in a hug.

"And, you know... sex too," came Fred's voice.

Julia laughed. "Obviously."

Ivy stood for a moment longer then slipped into her bedroom, closing the door with a quiet click.

On her laptop, she started browsing local properties. Maybe one would jump out at her. Maybe.

***

The next morning, Julia was making a pot of fresh coffee when Ivy went into the kitchen. Her dark hair was pinned up neatly and her make-up was as perfect as always. But there was tension in her jaw.

"Morning," she said, chirpily.

Ivy slipped into a seat at the island. "Hey," she said.

She had fallen asleep looking at depressing and pokey little apartments on her laptop and woken up with a really stiff neck from being in an awkward position, the screen still open next to her face.

"Fred here?" she asked, trying to sound casual.

"No," said Julia pouring out the coffee. "He's gone over to his brother's. Something to do with a blocked drain."

"Oh right," said Ivy. "So... erm..."

Julia set a coffee in front of her then sat down, the unnatural cheer falling away. "Ivy," she said, "I'm so sorry about yesterday."

"It's okay," said Ivy. "Honestly. Fred was right. I've been here for too long. You guys need your space."

"I've enjoyed having you here," Julia insisted. "And I think if you're not ready to move on then you shouldn't have to. I promised you this is your home for as long as you need it. I meant it."

Julia got up and fetched croissants from the bread bin and set them out on a tray in front of Ivy, then busied herself getting butter and jam. Ivy picked up a croissant and ripped a piece off, chewing it as Julia fetched what she needed.

"Julia?"

"Yeah?"

"Why don't you want me to... embrace the inevitable?"

Julia put down knives and side plates next to the croissants, butter and jam, then slipped back into her seat. "Honestly?"

"Yes."

Julia looked shifty as she spread blackcurrant jam across a piece of pastry. "You guys have been married for five years," she said. "Five years! Me and Fred, we've not even been married for two yet, and..."

"What?"

"I saw you making your vows, Ivy," she said. "I saw the love and the truth in those vows. And he fucking trampled them with absolutely no respect."

"Yeah," agreed Ivy. "He did."

"I hate that people can give up on their marriages so easily," she said. "If there's no hope for you then... what does that mean about my marriage? Is it all meaningless? Do those vows mean nothing?"

"Hey, Julia," said Ivy. "Are you saying you're glad I'm depressed because it gives you hope that Fred would be depressed if you left him?"

"What?" cried Julia, then her face went thoughtful. "Oh. Erm, I guess it does seem that way."

Ivy laughed. "Great, thanks."

"Sorry," said Julia, smiling guiltily. "It's pretty selfish really. I didn't think about it that way."

Ivy smiled. "There's nothing selfish about you at all."

"I just don't want my marriage to feel as meaningless to Fred as yours felt to Steven."

"It wasn't always meaningless," said Ivy sadly.

Julia had been right. Their vows had meant something when they said them. She remembered Steven's eyes when he'd promised to love her forever. There had been tears in them, real tears he tried to hide, not performative for the pleasure of the audience. During their first dance he'd held her close as Jason Mraz sang "I'm Yours", and he'd whispered in her ear that he loved her. Then they'd kissed, before he spun her round and caught her again, and they had laughed with joy and excitement. He had looked happy. He had wanted her.

Their marriage had been real.

"I know," said Julia. "I'm sorry. That wasn't fair."

Ivy shrugged. "Jules," she said after a moment. "I think it's time I moved out."

"Oh Ivy, please don't let our stupid fight drive you away!"

"I'm not, I promise," she said. "But I think we're both keeping me here for unhealthy reasons."

Julia sipped her coffee. "I think you might be right," she said reluctantly.

"Plus, I hear the market is perfect for looking to move in this area," said Ivy.

"I heard that too," said Julia, nodding sagely.

They smiled at each other.

**

Ivy sat on her bed looking through apartment listings. Fred had performed sadness with noble aplomb when she'd told him she was going to be more active in seeking out somewhere to live, but since she'd been upstairs, she'd heard Foo Fighters blasting out from the speakers downstairs and Fred singing along enthusiastically.

She nodded along to the music as she looked at the floor plan for a grotty little place over a deli, when suddenly the air went silent. She heard knocks at the door and slipped off the bed, opening her door in time to hear Julia's tense voice coming from downstairs.

"What?" she heard Julia's voice come from downstairs as she opened her bedroom door. "What are you doing here?"

Ivy froze. Julia sounded incredibly hostile. Who was it?

"Hello Julia," came Steven's voice. "How are you?"

Holy shit. No, it couldn't be Steven. It was somebody else. But that was his voice. It had to be his voice. She'd know that voice anywhere. But it couldn't possibly be. Could it?

"Hey there, Fred," came the voice again. Steven's voice. Definitely Steven's voice.

"Steven," said Fred, his voice as firm and harsh as Julia's.

Ivy felt herself start to shake. She crept out of the bedroom and onto the stairs, peering down towards the front door, trying to stay out of sight.

There he was, standing in the doorway, as handsome as the last time she'd seen him. Julia was standing between Steven and the living room like a tiny, and furious, guard dog. Fred was behind her, his hand on her shoulder, probably making sure she didn't punch him.

"What are you doing here?" Julia demanded.

"I was told that Ivy is staying here."

"Told by who?" Julia demanded.

"Helen Murphy," said Steven.

"Who the fuck is Helen Murphy?" snapped Julia.

"I used to work with her," said Ivy, coming down the stairs. "She came into the restaurant the other day and I told her."

The three faces at the door all looked at her. Steven held her eye contact. His expression was hard to read but Ivy thought he looked pleased to see her.

"Hello, Steven," she said.

"May I come in?" he asked her.

"Absolutely not," snapped Julia, turning back to stare at Steven.

"Julia," said Fred, quietly in her ear.

"I just want to talk," Steven said to Ivy, looking over Julia's head towards her.

"It's not my house," said Ivy.

Fred took Julia's hand and pulled her gently away from the doorway. Julia narrowed her eyes at Steven then turned to Ivy. "Up to you," she said.

Ivy nodded. "We can talk in my room," she said.

Steven squeezed into the room, Julia giving him as little space as she could manage, then followed Ivy. She didn't look back as she climbed the stairs, her mind racing. Why was he here? What did he want? Had she left underwear on the bedroom floor? Bollocks. This was not supposed to happen. She'd just decided to move on with her life. Why was he here?! Why now!? What did he want?!

Chapter Fourteen

Steven followed Ivy into her bedroom. She hastily kicked a pair of knickers under the bed before closing the door behind them. Not that he hadn't seen her knickers before, of course, but now it felt different. It felt awkward and violating to allow him to see her private things.

She stood with her back against the door, putting as much physical space between herself and her husband as she could.

Deep breaths. Deep breaths.

She didn't know what he wanted, but she knew she didn't want to be close to him when he told her.

"Ivy," he said. "I... I'm sorry."

Her heart was banging. Her hands were sweating.

"You are?" she asked. Her voice was barely above a breath. Her brain was foggy.

"I am," he said. "I was a fool. I can't believe I treated you that way."

Ivy shook her head, frowning. This wasn't what she was expecting. She didn't know what she was expecting but it wasn't this. She had to sit down, she felt wobbly.

Ivy walked past Steven and sat on the bed. Steven smiled and approached her, but Ivy held up a hand crossly. "I know this is a bed, Steven, but don't take this as a come on. I just needed to sit down."

"Fine," said Steven, holding up his hands and taking a step back.

"What do you mean, exactly?" she asked.

"I mean I'm sorry," he said.

"But what about? Why are you here? What do you want?"

"The way I treated you," he said. "And I'm here because I want to tell you that."

Ivy felt herself getting angry. "I haven't seen you in months, Steven!" she said hotly, standing up again. "Months! I'm your wife and you just fucking vanished as if I was a one night stand you picked up in a night club! I haven't heard from you! You blocked me on fucking Facebook! Now suddenly you decide to come here from... well... from wherever you're living because I obviously don't know where the hell that is... just to tell me you're sorry? What does sorry even mean? What are you sorry about? Are you sorry about leaving, or being a twat, or taking away my home, or making me feel like shit, or having no fucking soul?"

"Yes," he said. "All of it."

He looked at Ivy with such serenity. What was he so calm about!? What was he thinking?! Ivy felt herself crumble. The anger and frustration and rage were giving way to the heartache and desperation she had felt for months.

"Why?" asked Ivy, her voice quiet and confused and full of the pain she wished she was better at masking.

"Are you going to make me say it?"

Ivy stared at him. "Make you say what?"

Steven sighed and crouched down in front of her, squatting with his elbows on his knees, looking up at her. "You're right," he said. "I deserve the punishment."

"What punishment?" she cried. "What are you talking about!?"

"Ivy Rhodes," he said, reaching up and taking her hand. Ivy let him, though she didn't know why. She was just too

confused and overwhelmed by the whole experience to
object. "Will you... be my wife... again?"

Ivy's mouth fell open in shock. *What the actual...?*

Steven stood and cupped her face, pushing his lips onto
hers. *NO! STOP IT!* Ivy thrashed, pushing him away from
her with her hands and her feet, then wiping her face with
her arm. How dare he?!

"What the hell do you think you're doing!?" she
screeched, pushing herself backwards away from him,
pulling her knees to her chest.

"I love you, Ivy," he said, his voice cracking with
disappointment and hurt, standing away from her and
looking hopeful and earnest and desperate.

No, he didn't get to guilt her into kissing him. Not after
everything.

"You have a fucking funny way of showing it!"

"Tell me what you want, and I'll do it," he said,
dropping onto his knees in front of her, staring up again
with puppy dog eyes that begged forgiveness and love.
"Anything at all, Ivy. Anything."

Ivy was incredulous. She wondered momentarily if she
was able to conference call her mother, Julia and Mya and
get some advice. But even if it was possible, she
rationalised she'd end up in such a heated debate that it
wouldn't help anyway.

"What do you want, Ivy?" Steven asked again.

"You're asking what I want?" asked Ivy, rubbing her
head. What did she want? "What I want is to know why
you left! What I want is to understand how you could treat
me like that, and then what I want is to know why you
came back now!"

Steven stood up. "May I sit?"

"Sure," said Ivy, gesturing to the bed then moving away from him again.

Steven sat on the bed and patted the space next to him. Ivy looked at him incredulously, and he sighed.

"Fine." He rubbed his temples for a moment. "Ivy, sometimes my life it... it gets too much. I felt swamped and, I'm ashamed to say, I blamed you."

"Why?"

"We had been talking so much about trying for a baby," he said.

Ivy growled inside. HE had been talking about it. HE. She hadn't. She hadn't been ready and she'd told him that a thousand or more times!

"And moving to a bigger place," he went on.

HIM! She hadn't wanted to move; she'd been fine where they were. She'd also not needed the bigger TV, the bigger car, or the fancy kettle that lit up and had fifty buttons to press just to make a cup of coffee.

"And it just got too much," he finished.

Ivy took a deep breath. *Don't scream. Focus. He'll only back out and refuse to engage if you tell him everything you're upset about. Don't overload him. What's the most important thing you want to know?*

"So, why didn't you talk to me?" she asked. If he had, she could have told him, reassured him that the pressure to do all those things was all in his mind. She could have helped, been there, understood what was happening in his head and helped him understand what was happening in hers.

"It was the wrong choice," he said.

"You think?" snapped Ivy.

"My point is," he said. "I'm ready for it now. I'm ready to talk, to make a baby, to have the beautiful big home."

I'm not! I'm not! I'm not!

"I'm here, Ivy," he said. "I'm in."

"I think you're meant to be 'in' when you say I do," said Ivy, darkly.

"Ivy..."

"Steven," she interrupted. "I'm not the same person I was."

"Why not?"

"I want different things."

"Like what?"

Ivy chewed her lip. She'd been trying to deny her truth to herself, telling herself it wasn't practical, telling herself she was happy to embrace the circumstances she found herself in, but there it was, niggling away in her mind. She could have what she actually wanted.

She looked at him. He was gazing up at her with an earnest expression as if he really wanted to know the truth, but she had no reason to trust Steven with her hopes and her dreams. No reason to consider he'd respect them or understand them. He'd proved he couldn't be trusted. He'd proved he didn't care, or respect, or understand. If she started talking, he'd tune out. He always did. Her wants weren't relevant before, why would they be now?

But he was her husband. And she was in love with him, wasn't she? If anyone should hear her truth, it had to be him.

"I've had a look online. There are classes at the college here to make up what I missed from my degree," she said. "I could graduate, then go and get my Masters. I could finally be an architect."

"Is that what you want?" he asked, he sounded more surprised than Ivy thought was fair.

"Of course it is!" said Ivy. "It's what I always wanted, Steven. How could you not know that?"

"But you seemed so happy in your job," he said.

"I was never happy in my job!" she cried. "Ever! I did my job because we needed the income while you were training!"

"Oh."

"Oh?"

"I didn't realise," he said.

Ivy stared at him in silence for a moment. How could he possibly not know that?

"Do you know what degree I was doing when you met me?"

"Well, yes, but I didn't realise you still had ideas about that."

"I literally dreamed of being an architect from the day you met me! This wasn't supposed to be my life?! How little do you know me!?"

"But if that's what you want," he said. "Then that is what you should have."

"I agree," said Ivy, nodding firmly.

"So," he said, holding out his arms to her. "What do you say? Shall we make another go of it?"

Ivy turned away from him. She had to think. She couldn't look at him, it confused her.

She'd wanted this so much. She'd put off moving on with her life because of how much she'd wanted this. She'd lain awake at night, picturing his face, imagining him coming to her to apologise and beg her forgiveness. She'd imagined falling into his arms and holding him, smelling his neck, and being together again finally.

But now?

"Ivy?" asked Steven, standing up behind her and putting a hand on her shoulder, turning her around to face him.

"Do I have to decide right now?" she asked,

"No! Of course not!" Steven said, stepping back from her apologetically. "You need time. I respect that. How about we meet for coffee tomorrow?"

Ivy looked into his eyes. She saw the hope in them and remembered the emotion and love in them on their wedding day; the way they had crinkled with laughter when they'd eaten Chinese food from the top of the box; the exhausted bags beneath them when he'd done a twelve-hour-shift and finally lay down in bed next to her, cuddling into her before falling asleep. Steven's eyes.

"Sure," she said. "Tomorrow."

"Eleven thirty?" he said. "Hamlets?"

"Okay," she said.

Steven nodded. "Thank you," he said and went to leave, but turned at the last moment. "Ivy," he said. "I respect your boundaries, but, perhaps, a hug?"

He held his arms out to her.

"Okay," she said. *Why not?*

He walked to her and put his arms around her. At first, she was tense, stiff, but... then the familiar smell, the slightly sandpapery scratch of his cheek against hers, the soft but firm feeling of his chest against hers. She felt herself softening, allowed him to snuggle into her, and she snuggled back.

He sniffed deeply into her hair, then released her.

"I'll see you tomorrow, Ivy," he said. "Remember this, I love you."

Ivy went to speak, autopilot more than anything, to tell him she loved him too, but he put a finger to her lips. "Shh," he said. "Save it. We'll talk tomorrow."

Steven took his finger away and left her standing there, stunned. He closed the door on her, and she blinked.

What just happened?

***

The next morning, when Ivy had showered, dressed nicely, and applied more make-up than she cared to confess, she headed downstairs.

She'd stayed out of the way after Steven had left, not wanting to face any questions she didn't have answers for, and Julia hadn't come prying, which Ivy was grateful for. She had needed time to think.

When she'd emerged from the bathroom before going to bed, she'd found Julia and Fred casually admiring one of the paintings on the landing and they'd jumped like jacks when she'd opened the door. They had enquired about what Steven had said, and she'd told them about the coffee plans and why they were meeting, but as for opinions being expressed, even Julia had remained fairly silent.

Ivy suspected Fred had bribed or threatened her into not applying any pressure, but when Ivy went into the living room that morning, Julia was sitting in the armchair like a Bond villain, glaring, with Mya sitting on the coffee table next to her.

"What time's this shit show starting then?" demanded Mya.

"Well, hello to you too, Mya," she said. "And Dr No, you look well."

"Morning," said Mya.

"Fred at work?" asked Ivy.

"Yes," said Julia. "He tried to get out of it but there was a meeting he had to attend."

"So?" demanded Mya, standing up and stalking after Ivy as she headed into the kitchen.

"I'm meeting him for coffee at eleven thirty," she said.

"Just coffee?" asked Mya, closing in on her with Julia close behind.

"And conversation," said Ivy, filling the kettle with water.

"And possible reconciliations?" asked Julia.

"She's not going to reconcile," said Mya.

"You don't know that," said Julia.

"Are you?" asked Mya, looking at Ivy as she got the coffee pot out.

"I don't know," said Ivy.

And she didn't. She'd spent all night thinking about it. She'd swung between a categorical no, and a desperate and romantic yes. She felt overwhelmed with it all and sick to her gut at the prospect of either choice.

She'd remembered what felt like every second of their relationship. When they'd met at university, her playing pool with Mya and Mya's then-girlfriend Genevieve. How he'd come over to chat her up, tripped on the bag she'd left lying on the floor, landed on the pool table and potted the black. Mya had cheered him, and Steven had been so embarrassed he'd nearly chickened out of talking to Ivy. But he hadn't. He'd stayed, bought her a vodka and cranberry juice, and they'd talked for hours.

She remembered their first fight. They'd been to a party full of Steven's friends where Ivy didn't know anybody. He'd left her to go and do shots with some mates and she'd been so grateful when a man she knew from the history department came and chatted to her. Steven had been furious at her for not ignoring such an obvious come on, she had denied it and insisted they were just talking, but he told her she was the most beautiful woman there and of course he was hitting on her! She'd been infuriated and flattered in equal measure, and the fight ended in the first time they'd made love.

Their relationship hadn't been perfect, but Steven had always made her feel valued and wanted. At least, until recently.

"The guy's a scumbag," said Mya angrily.

"Bit harsh," said Ivy, drinking the coffee and trying to force her mind to settle and her heart to stop racing.

"And it's not like it's the first time he's fucked you over!" Mya raged on.

"Mya," said Julia softly, a hand on her arm, warning her to go gently.

"It isn't?" asked Ivy, putting her coffee on the side.

"Remember Paris?" said Mya, ignoring Julia's hand and carrying on.

"Erm..." Of course, she remembered. But she wasn't going to admit it. She shook her head. "No?"

"Yes, you do!" insisted Mya. "You lost your passport, and it was me and Theo who went round helping you get it sorted, visiting the police and the passport people, whilst the wonderful Steven stayed in bed with a hangover! He didn't even fucking text you!"

He'd been really ill; he could barely move without throwing up. How could he cope with scurrying around Paris over a mistake Ivy herself had made? Although she'd been so glad Mya and Theo had stepped up. She'd been so frightened and panicky, and Mya had been so helpful, and Theo was fluent in French. Really, without their help, she didn't know what would have happened. And Steven didn't even wake up until they had sorted it all out.

"Sure…" said Ivy, not making eye contact with Mya. "But he was ill. It happens."

"And didn't he pull something similar when you guys stayed in Liverpool?" said Mya, turning to Julia, who looked incredibly awkward.

"It wasn't exactly the same," said Ivy, really wishing she had stayed upstairs until it was time to leave.

She knew Julia could tell it was getting too much for her. The fury at Steven she'd been showing earlier had ebbed down and turned into for Ivy. "It was… different," she said, putting a hand on Ivy's arm and squeezing it gently.

Mya, on the other hand, was on a roll.

"He fucking abandoned you!" she cried, her arms flailing and nearly knocking the fruit bowl down. "Julia, don't go covering for him because you've got some happy-clappy Disney image of marriage you want to preserve in your head!"

"I'm not!" said Julia, defensive and cross. Ivy knew it was a bit too close to home for her.

"He left you on your own in the middle of the city because he got drunk and fucking forgot about you!" ranted Mya, leaning towards Ivy with a wild look in her eye. How long had she been holding onto this feeling of rage against Steven and not expressing it? "He fucked off to who knows where, with WHO KNOWS WHO, whilst you were in the goddamn pub bathroom!"

"Yeah," said Ivy, blinking. She put the coffee cup down carefully, her hands shaking. "He did."

Julia put her arm around Ivy, shooting a look at Mya. "It's okay, Ivy," she said. "You don't have to make decisions based on what anybody thinks except yourself."

"So, what are you saying?" demanded Mya. "You don't think she should actually get back with him?"

"No!" said Julia. "I think she owes it to herself to listen to what he has to say and make a choice based on her own relationship with him, not our anger towards him!"

"She needs to fucking move on is what she needs!" snapped Mya.

"They made a commitment to each other, Mya!" said Julia. "This isn't like your flings! She needs to give herself the time and the space to work out what it is she wants, not just quit because he messed up! Their marriage deserves at least a conversation!"

"Their marriage deserves the same respect he gave it!" said Mya. "As in, none at all!"

Ivy put her coffee cup in the sink and started to walk towards the door.

"She needs to be grown-up about this!"

Ivy picked up her handbag and put her coat over her arm.

"She needs to grow a bloody back bone and tell him to fuck off, like she should have done years ago!"

Ivy opened the front door. The sound snapped Mya and Julia out of their fight.

"Are you going?" asked Julia.

"Don't you need to work out what you're going to say first?" asked Mya.

"I think what I need is for other people to stop telling me what I need," said Ivy, looking at them seriously. "All I've been told for the last few months is that I need to get a job, and I need to go back to school, and I need to live at my mum's, and I need to get my own place, and I need to get back with my husband, and I need to move on." She took a moment and shook her head. "I think what I need is to not know what I need. Not right now. I'm going to live my life and then find out what I need, find out what I want. But I can't do that if everyone makes those decisions for me."

Her friends looked at each other sheepishly before coming towards her and wrapping their arms around her.

"Good luck, Ivy," said Julia, into the left side of Ivy's neck.

"Let us know what you decide to do?" said Mya, into the right side.

"I will," said Ivy, "and thanks."

Julia and Mya stepped back from her and she nodded before stepping out of the door and setting off to meet Steven to try and work out what it was she actually wanted.

Chapter Fifteen

Steven was already there when she arrived. He was sitting in the corner at a table with two mugs of coffee and two muffins on it. She wondered for a moment how long he'd been waiting and if the coffee in front of the empty chair was cold yet.

"Steven," she said, formally, as she approached him.

He smiled up at her then stood, coming round the table to embrace her and plant a firm but gentle kiss on her cheek. "Ivy," he said against her skin before moving away from her and smiling again. "Please, sit."

Ivy sat down and examined the blueberry muffin in front of her.

"I took the liberty of ordering for you," he said, as if she hadn't noticed. "Americano and a blueberry muffin, your favourite."

Your favourite. "Thank you," she said. "That's kind."

Ivy picked up the coffee, trying to stop her hands from trembling.

"Thank you for coming," he said. "I was worried you wouldn't."

Why did you order for me then? "You're welcome," she said.

"Ivy," he said, leaning towards her, a serious and intense look on his face. "I want to make you a promise. You said you want to make up the rest of your degree, right?"

"Yes."

"I promise you, Ivy Rhodes," he said, taking her hand. "Come back to me and I'll support you. You want to go for

your Masters? I'll support you. Whatever it is you want
and need, I will support you, Ivy. You deserve the life
you've always dreamed of, and I got in the way of that
once. I won't do it again."

She resisted the urge to take her hand away. They were
married. His touch was fine. She forced herself to focus on
his words instead of worrying about his touch.

His strong hands were wrapped around her own, his
thumb twiddling at her wedding ring which she'd never
taken off. She stared down at it for a moment, watching the
diamond reflecting the light overhead.

"How can I trust you?" she asked after a moment.

"Because I was wrong," he said, releasing her hand and
putting his own up in surrender. "And I'm sorry."

It was exactly what she had dreamed of. Exactly what
she wanted. For him to offer himself up to her like this. To
be able to study whilst he supported her, like she had
supported him. To be living with and loved by the man
she'd married, the man she'd built her future on. This was
what she wanted. What she'd always wanted.

"Please Ivy," he said, seeing her hesitation. "I promise
you. You can finally quit that ridiculous job and be a full-
time architecture student. Exactly what you always
wanted."

"I don't want to quit my job!" she said immediately.

It was a good offer, and she appreciated the sentiment
behind it, but she wasn't the same person anymore. She
valued her independence and freedom in a way she never
had when she'd been with Steven. If she gave up the job,
she'd be beholden to him entirely and, even if she had
trusted him not to leave her again, she knew she'd find that
too hard to cope with. Plus, she didn't want to stop working
at The Seven Seas. She liked it there. She liked the people.

"Why on earth not?" asked Steven, looking aghast. "Helen said you're dressed as a mermaid in a stupid wig!"

"Water nymph!" said Ivy, indignantly. "And I look good in that wig, thank you very much Helen!"

Steven raised his eyebrows. "I see."

"I don't want to quit my job," she said again. "I need my job. I LIKE my job. Not as much as I would like being an architect," she added quickly, seeing him raise his eyebrows. "But enough that I don't want to just leave it."

"Well," said Steven, shrugging. "If you're sure."

"I am," said Ivy. And she was. She was certain.

"So... what do you say?" he asked her. "I'm living in a great little apartment over the park. Room for two. Great views of the river."

She'd be stupid not to agree. He was supportive of her going back to school, and keeping her job at the restaurant, plus he seemed genuinely sorry, and it meant she could give Julia and Fred their space without moving into a dingy cellar flat with damp issues.

And she loved him. Of course.

She twiddled at her wedding ring, aware he was staring at her, a desperate hope on his face.

"Are you coming back to me, Ivy?" he asked her.

A home, an education, a relationship. These were the things she wanted. These were the things she'd always wanted.

"Come on, Ivy," he said.

What would Mya say? Would Julia be disappointed in her? Would her parents welcome him back into their lives?

"You know where you need to be," he said. "Come home to me. Let me spend the rest of my life reminding you why you gave me this second chance."

It wasn't about what Julia or Mya thought; it wasn't about her parents' opinions. It was about her. What did she want from life? A home, an education, her husband. Of course, those were things she wanted. It was logical. What was she waiting for?

"Okay," she said.

Steven flung his arms in the air in triumph, leapt from his chair and dropped to his knee next to Ivy, held her hand and kissed it, then stood and kissed her on the mouth, hard and full of passion and joy. Ivy let him.

"Right!" said Steven. "Eat your muffin and finish your drink, then I can take you to your new home!"

Ivy looked at the blueberry muffin and the cold coffee, then turned away and picked up her bag. "I'm not really hungry," she said, standing up and picking up her coat. "Let's just go, yeah?"

"Excellent!" said Steven as put his arm around Ivy's shoulders and steered her out.

He held onto her tightly as they walked, as if he was scared she was going to change her mind and run away. He wanted her and he loved her, and he treasured her. Just as she had always wanted him to do.

It wasn't far. A couple of streets over from Hamlets, in a quiet residential area. The apartment itself was beautiful. Far more luxurious looking than the home they had left.

"Wow," she gasped as he opened the door.

It was wide and spacious, with huge windows looking straight onto the river, floor to ceiling glass. The kitchen was small and neat, with expensive gadgets, and the television took up most of the wall.

"Let me show you around," he said.

He led Ivy down a small corridor.

"Bathroom," he said, gesturing to a door to the left, then to the right. "Bedroom."

He pushed the bedroom door open and Ivy went in.

"Wow," said Ivy again. "That's... a bed."

An enormous black leather sleigh bed was in the centre of the grey and white room. If beds could have testosterone, this one would be full of it.

"And very comfy," said Steven. "Take a seat."

Ivy perched nervously on the edge of the bed and gave it a little bounce. "Yep," she said. "Comfy bed. Of course, I suppose that's more to do with the mattress than the actual bed frame. Though maybe the support from the bottom contributes? I never really knew. In theory it would be better to invest money in a good quality mattress, rather than wasting money on the actual bed itself. Unless a good quality bed enhances the quality of the mattress? There's just so many things to factor in that I'd never really considered before. Maybe there's, like, some bed science to it and you need exactly the right combination of mattress to slat distance..."

Steven planted his mouth against hers, cutting her off mid nervous ramble.

She kissed him back. It was so familiar, but so strange, like kissing a memory.

He pushed his weight forward, forcing Ivy backwards onto the bed and lowering himself on top of her. He pressed against her, moaning slightly as his erection pressed into her thigh. Ivy's eyes widened. *Oh no!*

Get off, get off, get off, get off. She started to wiggle, patting him frantically on the arm. She couldn't breathe. He had to stop. His face was hot, his breath filling her mouth, his tongue squirming against hers.

"Oh yeah," he moaned, reaching his hands down to his trousers to undo them.

Ivy squealed and thrashed more, forcing her face away from him and taking desperate and panicked breaths. "STOP!" she cried out, smacking him on the arm even harder. "STOP IT!"

Steven pushed himself up and looked at her. "What?" he asked.

Ivy rolled away from him and stood up, backing away from him and straightening her hair and clothes, tears in her eyes.

"What's the matter?" he asked, his eyebrows furrowed.

"It's... too soon," she said, trying to force her voice to stop shaking.

Steven sat on the edge of the bed, like Ivy had before, pain on his face. "But... we're married."

"I just... I need... I need time!" said Ivy. "I can't just..."

Steven stood, his hands raised in submission and took a step towards her. "You're right," he said. "I'm sorry. We can take it slow."

"Thank you," said Ivy, nodding and easing herself backwards until her back was pressed into his bedroom door.

"I've just missed you so much and you're so very beautiful," he said, putting his hands down and taking a step towards her. "I just couldn't help myself."

He took another step.

"Steven..." she said.

He stepped towards her again and took her hands in his. She let him. She didn't know what else to do. She had nowhere else to go. The doorhandle was digging into her lower back.

"I'm sorry," he said again, looking into her eyes with a hunger. "I promise we will go at your pace. I promise. And I respect what you're saying. I know women can be weird about sex. Just know that... as soon as you're ready... I'm going to make you scream."

Ivy gulped.

"Why don't we go and get your stuff," he said, dropping her hand and reaching around her to open the bedroom door. "You'll feel more relaxed with your things here."

"Yeah," said Ivy slipping out from under him and following him out of the door. "Okay."

At Julia's, Fred carried her suitcase downstairs while Ivy followed him, feeling sheepish, with bags slung over her arms.

Julia sat perched on the arm of the sofa, a stony look on her face, as Steven loitered by the open front door.

"What did Mya say?" she whispered to Julia as Fred handed the case over to Steven to carry out to the car.

"Cunt," said Julia.

"Ah," said Ivy.

"She'll be fine," she said. "Don't worry about Mya. Just promise me that this is what you want?"

Ivy nodded and gave Julia a hug. "Absolutely."

Whispering in her ear, Julia said, "And if he fucks you over again, you come straight back here, got it?"

"Got it," said Ivy, and kissed Julia on her cheek.

"Ready Ivy?" asked Steven, coming back to the door.

"Ready," said Ivy.

Julia gave her hand a squeeze and Ivy wanted to hold on to her, but she squeezed back then went to Steven's side.

Fred approached Steven and held out a hand. "Steven," he said.

"Fred," said Steven.

They shook, then Fred nodded abruptly before turning to Ivy. "It's been lovely to have you," he said and held out his arms.

"Thank you, Fred," said Ivy. "I'm truly grateful for everything you've done for me."

He kissed her cheek then stepped back to let Julia through.

Julia pulled Ivy into another really tight hug, then released her and waved, wiping tears from her cheeks as Ivy followed Steven out to the car.

As Steven backed the car out of the driveway, Ivy waved goodbye to Julia and she reminded herself this wasn't the last time she would be seeing her. Just because she was moving out it didn't mean anything had to change.

"Are you alright, there?" Steven asked as they drove.

"Yeah," said Ivy, gazing out of the window.

They sat in silence as Steven drove her back to his home. Her home now, she supposed.

That night Steven opened a bottle of champagne, then they sat on the floor and ate Chinese take away straight from the cartons from the top of the coffee table.

"Remember that protest march you got us caught up in?" said Steven, grinning.

Ivy snorted into her drink. "Of course!" she laughed. "And don't pretend you didn't enjoy it."

"Oh, sure," he said. "The marching was fun; the strange fella next to me had quite a distinct odour though."

"Oh shush," said Ivy. "They were good people."

"Do you even remember what we were protesting?" he asked, offering her the spring rolls.

"The environment," said Ivy.

"We were protesting... the environment..."

"Oh, you know what I mean!" Ivy laughed. "DESTRUCTION of the environment."

"Are you sure?" asked Steven, laughing.

Ivy thought about it. "No," she said.

Then they creased with laughter and Steven refilled her glass.

After dinner they sat together on the floor, leaning against the sofa, and watching old episodes of Friends. Steven put his arm around her and cuddled her in close. It was comfortable, it was easy. It was almost like the months apart had never happened.

"I've missed you, Ivy," he said.

"I've missed you too," she said and smiled up at him.

Gently, he put his hand on her cheek and put his mouth against hers. Comfortable. Easy.

She kissed him back. He moved her, lowered her onto the carpet and pressed himself against her. Comfortable. Easy.

She let him start to pull her t-shirt up as he kissed her neck. His fingers crept up her body to her bra, then slipped inside and his fingers found her nipple. He groaned.

He pinched her nipple and it hurt.

This wasn't right. It was too soon. She couldn't stand it. The feeling of his hands on her, the grabbing, the pawing. She whacked at his arm but he didn't stop. *I'm not ready!!!*

"Steven!" she gasped.

"Ivy," he groaned.

"No! Steven, stop!" she cried, scrabbling to get out from underneath him. She pushed him and he rolled off her as she scooted herself away from him backwards across the carpet, breathing frantically.

He sat back, looking at her like she'd smacked him. "What?" he asked. "What happened? I thought... I thought you were into it."

"I was," she said, getting up off the floor and pulling the material of her bra back over her breasts. "I was I... I just..."

"What?"

"I couldn't breathe," she said. "I... I think... I still need time, Steven, I'm sorry."

Steven took a moment then nodded. "It's fine," he said, picking up the remote and turning off the TV. "Shall we go to bed? No funny business, just sleep."

Ivy nodded. "Thank you," she said.

While Steven was in the bathroom, Ivy quickly got changed into her pyjamas, then slipped under the grey duvet that lay across the oppressively masculine bed.

She listened to him flushing the toilet and brushing his teeth as she stared up at the ceiling.

This was her home now. She lived here.

Steven was flossing now. She knew his evening routine. It never changed.

She lay on her side and looked at her open suitcase leaning against the wall. She decided she should probably unpack soon. That would help.

As Steven opened the bathroom door and turned off the light, Ivy clamped her eyes shut.

Chapter Sixteen

Over the next few days Ivy drove over to her parents'
house after work and fetched a few boxes of belongings at a
time. No need to rush.

"I think you're very brave," her mother had said on the
first trip as she helped Ivy bring some things down the
stairs.

"Brave?" asked Ivy.

"Trusting him again," she said.

"Oh," said Ivy.

"Are you sure this is what you want?"

"Yes," said Ivy. "I'm sure."

Her mother had smiled at her, then tucked some of Ivy's
hair behind her ear, resting a hand on her cheek.

"I'm fine, Mum."

"I know you are, darling," she said. "But I'm your
mother and I worry."

"I know."

Steven was working long hours at the hospital, so Ivy's
life was suddenly very quiet again. She'd forgotten what it
was like to be home alone for any real length of time. She
was so used to having to seek out solitude, her parents'
presence being somewhat intrusive at home, and her own
presence being intrusive at Julia's. Now solitude presented
itself to her daily.

Her new routine was to come home from the restaurant,
take a shower, then unpack a box. She would watch some
television, drink a glass of wine, and try to make Steven's
apartment feel homely.

For Steven's part, he had stopped trying to push her for sex. He would offer her a kiss goodbye in the morning, and a kiss on the cheek when he got into bed next to her at night, if he thought she was awake. They had settled into a comfortable routine. They were living together amicably. It worked.

But the more Ivy thought about it, the more she knew it wasn't what she wanted. She needed more. She was ready.

***

Walking into the college, Ivy felt her heart start to bang. Her meeting with the admissions officer was in fifteen minutes and she was terrified, but deliriously excited too. She smoothed out her shirt and looked around nervously as an awkward-looking teenager with a bar through his nose shuffled past her.

She hadn't told anyone yet, not even Steven. She wanted to be sure it was possible, sure she was able to do this, before she announced it to the world. For now, this was just for her.

"Ivy?" asked a blonde woman with a large smile, stepping out of an office as Ivy sat nervously on a bench.

"Hi," said Ivy, standing up and holding out her hand.

"Stephie," said the woman, taking her hand and shaking it warmly. "Come on in."

Ivy followed her into the tiny office and they sat together as Stephie went through Ivy's paperwork and computer records.

"Well, you're really close to completing this degree," she said.

"Yes," said Ivy, her fingers twisting painfully as she forced herself not to start babbling, agitated nerves rattling around in her and threatening to burst out.

"What made you drop out?" asked Stephie as she clicked some buttons on the computer screen.

"I... my... my husband..." she said, suddenly panicking. She hadn't thought this bit through. "He... didn't..."

Stephie looked away from the screen and nodded with a gentle smile. "I understand."

"But I'm ready now," she said, desperately hoping she wasn't being judged as unworthy of completing her degree because she had let a marriage interfere with her career plans. *Can they turn people away for lack of feminist credentials?* Ivy wondered if she ought to talk about Caroline Criado-Perez or bell hooks to prove she was a strong and independent enough woman to join the course. Were architects meant to be very feminist?

Stephie smiled at her. "Then let's get you enrolled," she said.

Okay... maybe panicking that she wasn't a feminist enough architect student had been a little bit of an over-reaction. "Thanks," said Ivy, breathing a sigh of relief.

That night, Steven finished early and came home while Ivy was still cooking dinner.

"Steven!" she said, her voice squeaking a little as he waved to her before hanging his coat on the hook by the door. She hadn't expected him yet and she hadn't finished preparing her speech.

"Hello, darling," he said as he flopped onto the sofa. "Is there any of that Merlot left?"

Ivy nodded and went to the cupboard to get him a glass. Then refilled her own at the same time.

She glanced over at him, sprawling on the sofa and fishing around for the remote control. She'd have to tell him. He'd be fine. He had said he'd support her and that he was completely fine with it. She was only doing what they'd agreed to when they had got back together. It's not like it would be a shock. He had to know it was coming.

She carried the two glasses round the end of the counter, into the living room area and handed his to him. He smiled at her gratefully and took the glass.

"What are you making back there?" he asked her.

"Spaghetti," she said, going back to the stove where the water was starting to bubble.

"Oh," came Steven's disappointed voice behind her.

"And I've got sausages in the oven for you to have with it," she said.

"Thank fuck," came Steven's voice. "I dunno how you get by without at least a bit of flesh with your meal."

"I do fine," said Ivy, stirring the sauce. "So... erm..."

Steven came over to her and refilled his glass. "Yes?"

"I sorted my enrolment out today," she said. "At the college."

"Oh, well done," said Steven. "I was wondering if you were going to bother with that."

Ivy blinked. "Well, yes," she said. "I just have to retake the final year. It's evening classes so I'm going to talk to Ben about letting me just cover the day shifts."

"Evening classes?" he said, screwing up his nose. "Why don't you just ditch that job and do the classes during the day, then you can have your evenings free."

"No, it's fine," she said. "The classes I'm on are always evening, they're designed for people with jobs," she said. "It's all mature students, so I'm not going to feel like some old weirdo. And I can fit in the work on projects and things around the shifts the rest of the time."

"I see," said Steven. "And, what about us?"

"You work evenings all the time," said Ivy. "It's not really going to change how much time we spend together. It'll only be the occasional night when our schedules don't match. I'm sure we can make it work."

Steven looked like he was going to argue but he changed his mind. He nodded then took his wine back to the sofa and put the news on the TV.

Ivy put the spaghetti into the boiling water and glanced over her shoulder at the back of Steven's head.

***

Ivy got lost on the way to her first class. She arrived late and was dying inside as she slipped inside the classroom.

"Rhodes?" asked the teacher, looking over at Ivy.

Ivy panicked. Was she going to be told off? Oh god. It was high school again.

"Yes miss!" said Ivy. "I mean. Mrs..." Oh god... what was her name? She hadn't been in education in a very long time, what was she meant to do?

"Gloria Clarke," said the teacher, holding out a hand to Ivy and shaking it firmly. "Don't panic, I was just checking you were in the right classroom. There's a spot next to Olivia over there."

Ivy slipped into a seat next to a woman in her sixties who smiled at her warmly. "Olivia Telford," she said, holding out her hand.

"Ivy Rhodes," said Ivy.

They were a mixture of men and women, aged from their twenties to a gentleman in his eighties named

Bernard, who declared he was "collecting degrees". They smiled at her in greeting, then turned back to Gloria Clarke, who began her introduction again, for the sake of Ivy.

Ivy settled back in her seat. This was where she belonged.

Soon Ivy found herself racing through her day to get to her evening classes. She developed the utmost respect for her teacher and was delighted to work on the projects she assigned. Gloria Clarke was passionate about her subject and seemed excited to inspire her students. Ivy had worried that the evening classes would be taught by someone less committed, someone who felt mature students had just not bothered and therefore weren't worth bothering with. But not Gloria Clarke. She cared and she believed in her students' potential. She worked at a successful firm in London and had gone part-time to make room for educating the next generation.

Ivy felt fulfilled in a way she hadn't felt in a very long time.

Her fellow classmates became some of her favourite people to mix with. They were diverse and interesting, and they all cared as much as she did about getting their degrees. Each one was on the mature student course for a different reason, and they were all loving their experience.

Ivy found herself stimulated and interested, challenged and excited. She started drawing again, and realised she hadn't even tried in years, and how much she'd missed it. She despaired for herself at the years she had wasted not putting time into this subject that she loved so much.

Working at the restaurant in the day before heading to the college left Ivy exhausted but happy. If she was home before Steven, she was usually fast asleep by the time he got there and, on the days she was home first, he kept to himself to give her space to work, her papers and books filling the coffee table.

They were like passing ships, but he had promised he understood that it mattered to her and to support her, and it was only for a year. It was worth it. It would make their relationship stronger in the end because it would mean Ivy was finally happy. And, right now, she was the happiest she could remember being. She was becoming the person she wanted to become.

One Tuesday, after she'd been studying at the college for about a month, Ivy saw Mya and Julia approaching her podium at The Seven Seas excitedly.

"Ivy!" they cried, and both threw their arms around her.

"Guys!" said Ivy. "It's been so long!"

"You're so busy," wailed Mya. "We figured we'd have to catch you here if we were going to see you."

"Do you have a break coming up?" asked Julia.

"I'll see if Daisy can cover me for ten minutes," she said. "I'll put you down at the bar, yeah?"

Ivy watched her friends head through the restaurant and round the massive whale, then turned and greeted a family of five that were in the line behind them. On the way back from seating them, she called Daisy over to cover her, then headed to the bar to talk to her friends.

"So, tell us everything," said Julia, perched on a bar stool, cocktail in hand. "How's school? How's work?"

"How's Steven?" asked Mya, her eyes sharp.

Ivy hesitated.

"Everything's great," she said. "Seriously. Managing both working and school is a challenge, obviously, but Ben's being super flexible and supportive. If I need to move shifts around, he's doing everything he can; it's really cool of him. And college is amazing - my teacher's, like, this incredible woman who has done so much stuff and knows... well... everything!"

They looked at her. Waiting for her to go on. She knew they wanted a Steven update.

"And Steven's..." she took a moment. What should she say? "Wonderful!" she settled on.

"Oh?" asked Julia, almost casually.

"So supportive," she enthused, nodding earnestly. "Really understands how much this means to me. Totally gets it. He's brilliant. I mean OBVIOUSLY he's brilliant, that's why I went back to him because he's my Steven, and he's smart, and handsome, and fun, and very supportive. So happy for me. Obviously."

Mya and Ivy flashed each other a look.

"That's great," said Mya. "Glad to hear it."

Julia sipped her cocktail and didn't comment.

Behind the bar, the door to the office opened and Ben came out, carrying several folders of documents in his arms and looking busy, but when he spotted Ivy he smiled and came over.

"Oh, hello again," he said, noticing Mya and Julia as he set the folders down on the bar. "We met before, when I was a pirate."

"Captain Ben," said Mya, smiling with approval. "You make the non-pirate look work too."

"Well, I try," said Ben with a laugh. "Are you having another drink? On the house?"

"Then definitely," said Mya. "Three bottles of Champagne please!"

Julia whacked her on the arm. "Ignore her, we're on the Sea Breezes. Thank you!"

"Coming right up," said Ben, and busied himself behind the bar making the drinks. Ivy watched him move about for a moment before looking back to her friends.

Mya and Julia were watching her pointedly.

"What?" she said, glaring at them, knowing EXACTLY what.

"Hey, I'm not married!" said Mya, spinning a finger at her. "Turn that glare on yourself, young lady!"

Ivy felt her cheeks flush and when Ben brought the drinks back, she couldn't meet his eye.

"How's it going today, Ivy?" he asked her. "Seems busy."

"Yes," she said formally. "It is indeed very busy."

He made a confused face. "Do you want a coffee or anything whilst I'm back here?" he asked her. "Before I head back to the land of spreadsheets and marketing calls?"

"No thank you," she said. "I will be just fine. So no. But I appreciate it. Thank you." *Oh, just speak normally, Ivy you idiot.*

He laughed gently, confused by her tone. "Okay," he said. "I'll get one for me, then head back. Nice to see you again," he said to Mya and Julia.

Ivy sank into a seat next to Mya and silently loathed herself while Ben made his coffee, gave him an awkward wave as he left, then put her face on the bar.

"Ivy and Ben, sitting in a tree," said Mya in a sing-song voice.

"Not funny," she said, sitting up.

"K I S S I N G," sang Mya.

"I said, it's not funny!" snapped Ivy, then got up and walked away back into the restaurant, leaving Mya and Julia looking confused behind her.

She relieved Daisy and stood at the podium feeling foolish and stressed. When Mya and Julia came over after they'd finished their drinks, ready to apologise, Ivy shook her head.

"No, please don't," she said. "I'm so sorry. I'm so tired with working all the time and it's just..." *Just what? She had a crush on Ben? No, of course not! She was madly in love with Steven! Obviously!* "I'm just a bit fried. And I'm sorry. Are we okay?"

"We're always okay," said Mya, putting her arms around Ivy and giving her a hug.

Julia rubbed Ivy's arm as she hugged Mya, then took a turn hugging her herself.

"We'll catch up properly soon, yeah?" said Julia. "One weekend when Steven's working and you're not, we'll come round. Okay? Like the old days?"

"Definitely," said Ivy. "I've missed you guys."

She really had missed them. And it would be really nice to spend an evening relaxing with her friends rather than circumnavigating Steven's moods.

Chapter Seventeen

Ivy came home from college late one October evening, to find Steven sitting at the table in the kitchen eating curry, a white plastic bag of empty tubs on the table next to him.

"Oh yay," she said, dropping her laptop bag and going over. "What are we having? I'm starving!"

"I didn't know when you'd be home, so I didn't get you anything," he said, putting a piece of chicken in his mouth without looking up. "And it's all meat, so you wouldn't like what's in there."

"Oh," said Ivy, chronically disappointed but in too good a mood to let it show. She had got the marks from her first assignment that evening, and they were brilliant. She was proud and excited and full of positivity for life. Nothing could destroy that. "Don't worry, I'll just make a sandwich or something."

"Okay," said Steven.

"I had a great night at college," she said.

"Good."

"I got my first assignment back," she said, getting the bread and cheese and salad out.

"Good."

"Not just good," she said as she proudly built her sandwich up, noticing his sullen responses but committed to her joy. "I'd go as far as to say amazing."

Steven nodded, and ate another piece of chicken. Fine. She had plenty to be getting on with. She didn't need his validation.

"I'll go eat in the living room; I've got a ton of work to get on with," she said, picking the sandwich up.

"You've got to work?" he asked her, looking up to watch her walk away. "Now?"

"Yeah," she said, setting her sandwich down on the table. "It's a bit full on."

"I thought we could do something together," he said, setting his knife and fork down on the plate with a clang. "Maybe take a bath? Bit of music? Candles?"

The offer he made was full of romance. The tone he offered it in was not.

"That sounds great, but I've got a split shift at the restaurant tomorrow," she said, picking her laptop bag up again. "And I've got a project due in on Thursday, so I need to get on with it."

"Sure," said Steven. "I get it."

Ivy opened up her laptop and tipped some books out onto the sofa beside her, then settled herself cross-legged on the floor before taking a bite out of her sandwich. Soon she was deep into her work, and only noticed when she went to fetch a glass of water that Steven had vanished.

When she went to bed, Steven was already asleep. She lay down next to him and snuggled down. She was getting used to the clunky bed. At least the mattress was super comfy.

The next day at the restaurant, Ivy spotted Ben walking in, headed for the office, as she led a family to a table by a giant plastic lobster. She waved to him to wait, then, when the family were comfortably settled, she hurried back towards him with a huge grin on her face that she couldn't contain.

"You're in a good mood!" he said, laughing.

"Guess what, guess what," she said, literally bouncing with enthusiasm now.

"What?" he asked, a delighted expression on his face already.

"I aced my assignment," she said.

"Ivy!" he cried and held up a hand. She high-fived him. "That's bloody brilliant!"

"I know," she enthused. "I've got a massive project due in on Thursday which I've been stressing about, but this was a massive confidence boost!"

"Do you need any extra time for it?" he asked her. "I can move shifts around for you?"

"No, it's fine," she said. "Thanks. I'm fitting it all in so far."

"Well, that's awesome," he said, nodding. "I'm really pleased for you."

"Thanks," she said, smiling broadly.

Ben smiled at her, hesitated a moment like he wanted to say something else, then patted her on the arm. "I'll see you later, yeah?" he said. "Well done again."

Ivy smiled and watched him leave, before turning back to the podium as another family came in to be seated.

***

A few weeks after Ivy's assignment results, she finally had a Saturday night with no college pressure and no shift scheduled at the restaurant, that coincided with Steven working nights at the hospital.

"Jeez, it's like we're back at uni!" Ivy exclaimed with amusement as she let Mya and Julia in, and observed their arms heaped with take-away pizza, crisps, biscuits, sweets, cheap wine and vodka.

"Well, you ARE back at uni," said Mya, walking past her. "So, we figured we'd go old school."

Mya pushed Ivy's laptop aside on the coffee table and put the massive pizza box down, then looked around. Ivy realised it was the first time her friends had actually been inside Steven's apartment. A knot of guilt twisted inside her.

"Nice place," said Julia looking around as she followed Mya to the living room. "Kinda..."

"A bit..." Mya said.

"Stark?" asked Ivy as both of them tailed off. "I know."

"You've been living here a few months now, what gives?" asked Mya, flipping open the pizza box lid and taking out a huge slice. "Where're the Ivy touches?"

"Steven likes it this way," she said, shrugging.

Honestly, she could have decorated if she'd wanted to. She didn't think he'd have minded particularly. She just didn't want to. It didn't feel right.

"Fair enough," said Julia, ignoring the look Ivy saw Mya shooting at her. "Where's the wine glasses?"

"I'll get them," said Ivy heading to the kitchen cupboard.

"Ivy," said Mya, hopping up and down behind her, "Ask me about my job."

"How's your job?" asked Ivy, handing out wine glasses.

"It's fucking AMAZING," cried Mya, her face lighting up with glee. "I'm going to be travelling a bit, which is usually a pain in the arse, because they're doing a lot of location shoots," she went on. "But it's worth it. And they're an awesome crew, so it'll actually be brilliant."

"That's so good!" said Ivy, pouring wine into a glass and handing it to Mya. "I'm so proud of you!"

"Thanks," said Mya, accepting the wine then taking a big swig, before grimacing. "Oh Jesus, that's terrible."

"I wanted to make the experience authentic!" said Julia with a shrug before accepting her wine from Ivy.

"How's college going?" Mya asked Ivy. "Are you loving it?"

"So much," said Ivy. "I talked to Gloria, the teacher, about my Masters, and she's pretty certain if I keep these results up and do well in my final exams that I'll be able to get onto the course I want."

"Ivy, you absolute legend," said Julia. "Let's toast to this!"

"To Ivy and her massive brain!" said Mya, holding up her wine glass.

"To Mya and her amazing talents!" said Ivy, holding up hers.

"To both of you," said Julia. "And to me, because I paid for the wine and the pizza."

"To Julia!" said Ivy and Mya at the same time.

They laughed and toasted, then settled into an evening of laughing and catching up.

At eleven, the door opened, and Steven came in looking harassed. He saw them sitting around, drunk and laughing, and sighed heavily as he shut the door and dropped his coat and bag on the floor.

Ivy felt herself sober up suddenly, and she hurried to him. "Are you alright?" she asked.

"Yes," he said. "And you're busy. So, I guess I'll head to bed if there's no food."

"I thought you were going to eat there?" she said, nervous. "I told you the girls were coming round! I... I didn't think I needed to cook anything for you."

"Forget it," he said, walking away from her. "It doesn't matter."

"Steven, I'm so sorry," she called after him.

"Please don't make a scene, Ivy!" he snapped, turning to her sharply. "I'm a grown man. I can look after myself, if I have to."

He spun back around from her and stalked away and into the bedroom, closing the door behind him. Ivy chewed her lip then turned back to her friends, embarrassed.

"Come on Mya," said Julia. "Let's get stuff packed up and I'll call us a taxi."

"Oh, guys," said Ivy, hurrying over. "You don't have to go!"

"We know," said Julia, putting a hand on Ivy's arm. "It's fine. We're tired and it's late. And you guys obviously need a bit of space."

Ivy nodded. Steven would be grateful if they left. It was probably for the best.

After Mya and Julia had helped her clean up and headed out to their taxi, Ivy slipped into the bedroom and saw Steven lying in bed, facing away from her.

"Steven?" she whispered. But he didn't answer.

She was kind of relieved. She was far too tired and drunk for a fight. She climbed into bed and settled herself down. At least she'd had a fun evening with her friends.

When she woke up in the morning, Steven had already left.

***

"You look strange out of costume," said Ben as he poured a large glass of Shiraz.

"Charming!" laughed Ivy.

She and Ben were covering the bar staff who'd both called in sick, and that meant normal clothes, not fancy dress. If she was honest, Ivy felt strange being there without the face paint and scales, but she was definitely more comfortable in trainers, leggings and a Seven Seas t-shirt.

Ben handed the woman at the bar her drink and took the money, then grinned at Ivy. "I mean, I quite like it," he said. "It's just a bit weird to think of you as a human."

"It's weird to think of you at all," said Ivy, sticking her tongue out. Then she felt her cheeks burn. Oh, for the love of fuck, did she just tell Ben she thought about him? *Oh god. Back pedal! But how!?*

"I do appreciate you helping me," he went on. He seemed not to have noticed. She tried to calm the panic. "I covered this shift with Tia last time, but she got mojito in my eye."

Ivy laughed. "How!?"

"I dunno!" said Ben, holding up his hands. "But it stung like hell. I thought I'd go blind!"

Ivy laughed. "She's doing a good job up front," she said.

"Yeah, the scales suit her," agreed Ben. "I guess she'll move up there full-time when you leave us."

"Leave?" asked Ivy. "Are you firing me?"

"What?" gasped Ben. "No! Of course not! I mean, when you're qualified, I'm assuming you won't be an architect who moonlights as a mermaid."

"Water nymph," said Ivy.

"That too," he said, smiling sadly.

"I mean... yeah," said Ivy, frowning. "I guess I will be leaving one day."

When she had started at The Seven Seas, she had felt like she tolerated the job, accepted it for the money and the

security, but not dreamed of being there longer than she
had to be.

But now? It was her home away from home. It was
comfort and support and encouragement. It was laughter
and friendship and companionship. It was independence
and security. She was seeing her parents and her friends
much less often now that she was studying as well as
working, and it could easily become isolating and sad. But
she found everything she needed here, in this funny little
themed restaurant. What would she do without these
people? Who would she celebrate with, who would she
laugh with?

"Are you okay?" asked Ben, studying her face.

"Yeah," said Ivy. "Just... I hadn't really thought about
leaving. I'll miss it here."

"We'll miss you too," said Ben.

They stood for a moment, Ivy looking into Ben's eyes,
studying the disappointment that lived there.

"I've got time yet," she said, pulling her eyes away and
turning to pick up clean glasses and hang them over the
bar. "I've got to do my Masters yet! You'll get sick of the
sight of me before I leave here."

"Never," said Ben quietly, before smiling at a man who
had come to the bar.

"Amstel please, mate," said the customer.

"Coming right up," said Ben, going to the beer tap. "So,
is Steven super proud of you?" he asked Ivy as he
concentrated on pulling the pint.

"Yeah," said Ivy, nodding as she carefully slid the wine
glasses into the rack. "Totally."

"Cool," said Ben, nodding to himself. "Cool."

That night, Ivy was careful to make sure there was a
plate covered in sausages, bacon, home-made chips, mushy

peas and onion rings in the oven with a cover over them before she went to bed. She left a post it on the front of the microwave detailing what was in there and set the timer to the right time to heat it all up. Ivy hated the smell of bacon, but it was Steven's favourite and he always complained that he didn't get to eat it often enough.

In bed, she read one of her schoolbooks by the light of the bedside lamp until she heard the front door open, then she slipped the book onto the bedside table, turned out the lamp and closed her eyes.

A moment later, the bedroom door opened, and Steven peered in.

"Ivy?" he whispered.

Ivy didn't answer.

Steven closed the door again.

Chapter Eighteen

As the winter came and Christmas approached, Ivy started preparing for exams. She was finding this section of the syllabus a challenge and wanted to put as much extra time into revising and focusing as she could.

On her break at work, she sat by the bar, poring over a textbook and making notes.

"How's it going?" asked Daisy, who was working the bar that day.

"I suck," wailed Ivy, folding her arms and dropping her face down onto the book.

Daisy laughed. "Oh, come on," she said. "We all know you're smart."

Ivy sighed. "Thanks," she said. "I just need to get through this exam then I can relax over Christmas."

"Ha," laughed Daisy. "You work in a restaurant now, Ivy Rhodes."

Ivy smiled. "Trust me, working here is significantly less stressful than everything else in my life."

"Everything?" asked Daisy, raising an eyebrow.

"You know what I mean."

Ivy went back to her book for the last five minutes of her break, determined to get her head around this and nail the exams.

That night, she sat on the living room floor, making notes from the books and her computer, music on quietly, eating digestives straight from the packet and pounding yet another pint of coffee.

Steven came out of the bedroom and leaned on the wall, watching her. She glanced up at him and smiled before going back to her revision.

"Ivy," he said after a moment.

"Hmm?"

"Are you coming to bed?" he asked her.

"Soon," she said. "I just want to finish this chapter. It's boggling my brain and I really need to get a handle on it before class tomorrow."

She went back to her work, but Steven didn't leave. He stayed leaning on the wall, watching her.

"Ivy?" he said again.

"Yes?" she said, looking up at him.

"I want you to come to bed now," he said.

"I'm... working..." she said, gesturing to the notes and the books and the research that were occupying the table in front of her.

Steven stopped leaning on the wall and walked towards her, standing over her where she sat surrounded by notes. She looked up at him as he stood there, looming above her, a stern look on his face. "I work," he said. "I work in a hard job for long hours. But I still make time for my wife."

Ivy felt tears prick her eyes. She was exhausted; she was working non-stop and preparing for an exam she was stressed about. She was too tired to cope with a fight. She was too tired to emotionally handle Steven's apparent anger. But she had to work. She had to study. "I... I've got my exam..." she said quietly.

"And you have a husband," he said. "And you're going to come to bed with me now; we're going to make love, and then we're going to fall asleep together. Like husband and wife should."

Ivy felt her lip quivering. What was happening? She was so tired, so stressed. She was reading him wrong. She was certain she was reading him wrong. She felt the tears burning at her eyes.

Steven turned off the music and pushed her laptop shut.

"Now, Ivy," he said.

Ivy slowly stood up. He took her hand and led her into the bedroom. He undressed himself, then removed her clothes and lay her on the bed.

"I love you, Ivy," he said.

"I love you too," said Ivy.

Steven pressed himself on top of her, pushed himself inside her. Ivy let him. She didn't know what else to do.

When Steven went to sleep, Ivy lay on her side and stared at the wall.

***

Ivy was staring into space, her mind racing, as she stood at her podium at The Seven Seas Restaurant the next morning.

"Are you alright, Ivy?" came a voice next to her.

Ivy turned and saw Malcolm and Ben looking at her, their faces creased in matching concern.

"Yes," she said, blinking and focusing. "I'm fine. Sorry."

Ben glanced at his uncle then back at Ivy. "Sure?" he asked her.

"Yes, thank you," she said, putting a smile on her face.

She could tell they didn't believe her but they both accepted her at her word and walked back through the restaurant to the office. Ivy sent her enthusiastic smile after them, then turned back to face the door again.

Got to focus. Can't lose this job. Got to get a grip.

She was just so stressed about the exams. That was all. She knew they'd be hard. She knew it'd be a challenge. She had been putting everything into them and she was just a bit stretched. That was all. Exam anxiety. Everything else was fine. *Of course, everything else was fine. Why wouldn't it be?*

She had everything she had ever wanted.

***

On Saturday afternoon, Ivy frantically ran around the living room. She gathered cups and plates and carried them into the kitchen to go into the dishwasher. She plumped the sofa cushions that she'd bought the day before and arranged on the sofa. She straightened out the fluffy rug she'd bought too and rearranged the picture frames she had finally unpacked and displayed.

It was starting to resemble a home that Ivy would live in.

"What's the fuss?" Steven asked, sitting on the armchair, reading the paper, and watching Ivy as she scurried around.

"I've not seen them in weeks!" said Ivy as she ran a cloth over the mantlepiece. "And they've not seen this place yet."

"So?"

"So, I want it to be perfect."

"New cushions and an unnecessary rug make it perfect, do they?" asked Steven, turning the page and not looking up at her.

"No, I mean, sort of," said Ivy, shrugging.

"I'm surprised you had time for all this," said Steven, putting his paper on the arm of the chair and standing up.

"What?" asked Ivy.

"I mean, going out shopping for luxuries," he said, gesturing at the cushions. "Spending the day tidying. Feels a bit indulgent, doesn't it?"

"I bought a couple of things in Dunelm after work; I didn't spend the day swanning around in Chanel," she said, irritated. "And obviously I'm tidying up! My parents are coming!"

Steven leaned against the wall, his arms folded, watching her. She felt very self-conscious but ignored him. She had things to do, and his glare couldn't get in the way.

"Don't you have some studying to do?" he asked her after a minute.

For God's sake. "Yes," she said, as patiently as she could. "I have a lot to do actually, but my parents are coming. Like I said."

"And that Ben chap was fine with you having time off from the restaurant?"

She was going to throw one of the new cushions at him in a minute. "He was fine," she said. "I've worked all week, and he said I'm due a Saturday off."

Ivy headed into the kitchen to get a glass of water.

"So, you can take time off then?" he said, following her. "If you want to, I mean."

Ivy stopped and turned to him. "I guess so..." she said. His tone made her uncomfortable. His face was hard. "Why?"

"Just observing."

"Observing what?" asked Ivy, trying to stop her hands trembling as Steven stepped closer to her.

"You can put your work and your education aside to, say, plump pillows that your dad won't even look at before he sits on them, but if I'm working late you can't take time out to cook dinner for me."

"Excuse me?" said Ivy. "I cook dinner for you all the time!"

"No," he said. "You used to. Now you forget. Then you go overboard leaving bacon to congeal in the microwave for me, thinking that makes up for it, then you go back to forgetting about me again."

"I have to work too!" she protested. "And I cook for you as often as I can!"

"I've eaten take-out four times in the last week, Ivy."

Ivy stared at him. What was happening? Why was he doing this?

"So?" she said, eventually.

"So, you're my wife," he said, stepping closer to her. "And I deserve better."

I'm your wife so you're entitled to use me, you mean. Use me as a maid; use me as a sex toy. That's what you think you deserve. That's what you think a wife is.

Ivy felt herself get angry. He had snapped at her that he was capable of looking after himself when Mya and Julia were there but, what? Now he couldn't? Now, he was speaking to her like she was a naughty child who needed telling-off because she'd somehow failed him. She felt her temper flare.

"You're quite capable of cooking for yourself, Steven!" said Ivy, hotly. "What did you do for the months we weren't together? Did you get some other woman in to service your needs?"

"I don't think that's the point!" he snapped at her.

"I'm right!" she said, a realisation suddenly dawning on her. It made so much sense. "You did, didn't you. And she left! That's why you came back to me; that's why you waited that long, why it was then. That's what changed! You moved some other woman in and then, when she left, you decided I was the easiest replacement for you!"

"How fucking dare you," he snarled at her.

"Am I wrong?" she asked him, tears coming to her eyes. Anger and pain from his leaving, his return, his behaviour, suddenly flooding her. "Tell me I'm wrong. Because right now I feel fucking right."

Steven stormed towards her. "Do you have so little respect for me?"

Ivy panicked. The anger that had burned so powerfully was immediately flushed out by fear. He looked so angry. She tried to back away from him, but the room was so small. She had nowhere to go.

"I'm sorry," she said. "That wasn't fair. I... I'm just feeling under a lot of pressure right now."

"I see," he said. "So, you think it's fair to put pressure on me, do you? Ivy's feeling pressure, so the whole world has to stop and suffer with her. Because if Ivy's feeling something, that's the only thing that matters. It's all about Ivy."

"No, of course not! I just... I need to do well in my exams if I'm going to get onto the Masters course, and Gloria..."

"The Masters course," said Steven, interrupting her and rolling his eyes.

"Yeah," said Ivy, trembling. "I can get on if I do well in my exams and..."

"You're not still thinking you'll do a Masters?" Steven interrupted her.

"I... what?" she said. "Of course, I am."

"Look, Ivy," he said, his voice changing, becoming soft and understanding, patronising. "I said I'd support you - and I have - every step of the way. Despite everything you've put me through for this godforsaken little degree. But let's get real now."

"Get real about what?"

"You're nearly thirty-one, Ivy," he said. "This isn't time to pretend that your little hobby is more important than your life."

"Little hobby? I'm studying for my dream career!" she said, her voice cracking. "Not learning how to crochet!"

"Don't be deliberately obtuse, Ivy." He snapped at her; his voice harsh again. "You speak to me like I'm your father and you're a stubborn teenager."

Ivy blinked. Steven moved closer to her and she pressed herself against the sink, her heart hammering and her hands sweating.

"You are my wife," he said to her, now so close she could smell the coffee on his breath as he looked down into her face. "That means something."

"I know it does," she whispered.

"It's time for you to grow up. You'll finish your degree, so you can get your pride back or whatever, then we'll go back to getting our lives on track. You can get a job, a better job than this ridiculous thing you're doing now, of course..."

"What..." she spluttered, interrupting him. "I... I... But..."

"Ivy," he said.

"I don't want to do that!" she wept, "I don't want that. I'm going to be an architect!"

"Oh, come on. You can't expect to do a Masters and then start as a junior in some firm, at your age," he said, mocking her.

"Why not?"

"You're getting on now," he said. "It's a biological fact. You missed your chance for the career, so let's salvage what's left of you and make sure you have a baby before you're even too old for that."

"Why are you saying all this?" she cried.

Steven moved in, pressing himself against her, trapping her. She leant back away from him, her head hitting the cupboard behind her as she bent backwards over the sink, trying to keep her face away from him. Her body shook with fear. She could feel the blood pounding in her head.

She wanted to push him, fight to get away from him, scream at him, run from him. She wanted to knee him in the balls or grab a cup from the side and smash it over his head. She wanted to spit in his face or headbutt him. She wanted to. She wanted to fight.

He was so big. She felt dizzy. She wanted to fight. She wanted to.

"Do you realise we've only made love once since you moved back in here?" he whispered into her ear; his breath wet. "Once, Ivy."

She felt tears pouring down her cheeks as his hands gripped her arms, his body pressed against her own.

"And let's not kid ourselves," he said. "Your heart wasn't in it. I could tell. Do you really think I can enjoy making love to you when I can see you don't want to be there? When I see the disinterest in your eyes? You used to want me, Ivy. You used to long for me."

"Why did you do it then?" she whispered, through her tears. "If you knew I didn't want to. Why did you do it?"

"Because I know what I want, Ivy. I know what I want, and I go for it," he said. "Maybe I should start doing it more. You used to want me because I was in charge, but now? Now you don't need me in the same way. You don't see me as a man anymore."

"No!" cried Ivy.

"I can show you how much of a man I am," he said, pressing himself against her so hard that the edge of the sink was pressing painfully into her back, her neck twisted uncomfortably against the cupboard door, his fingers digging into her skin on her arms. "We can get our marriage back, Ivy."

"Steven, please," she wept. "Please, stop."

He released her left wrist and gripped her hair, turning her head to face him.

"I can be the kind of man you respect again," he said, then pulled her head to the side and started kissing her neck.

"Steven!" she cried out, frantically thrashing her free arm against him. She wanted to fight him off. She wanted to. "Steven, stop!"

"Why?" snarled Steven.

"I don't want this!" she cried out. She pushed him, hard and as he staggered back, surprised, she squirmed away from him, backing out of the kitchen.

He turned and followed her, his face red with anger.

"What?" he demanded. "What don't you want, Ivy? Our marriage? A baby? Me?"

"No! I mean..." Ivy tried to force herself to breathe more slowly. "I mean, maybe a baby, one day, sure, but now? I know what I want now! I want to get my degree. I want to do my Masters. I want to finally get my dream job! I want... I want to be happy, Steven."

"You can't be happy here? With your own husband?"

Ivy felt her heart race and her hands sweat and her knees wobble. But she knew what to say.

"No," she said, shaking her head. "I don't think I can."

"I gave you everything you wanted, Ivy," he said. "A home, support, love. I was ready to keep you safe, make sure you never had to go out to work again. I was your slave, Ivy! I did everything for you! What more could you possibly want?"

"I didn't ask for that life! I didn't ask for any of it!" she said. "I told you what I want! I told you why I was coming back. I didn't come here to change what I want!"

"But what about me, Ivy?" he demanded. "What about what I want? Does that mean nothing to you?"

"No but..." she said. "But I think... I think what I want means more."

"That's incredibly selfish," he said.

"Maybe," said Ivy, shrugging sadly. "But I deserve to be happy and... I'm not happy here, Steven. I'm not."

Steven turned away from her, picked up a mug, and threw it into the sink. It smashed, cold coffee and broken china thrown up into the air and splattering the counter and floor.

Ivy gasped, flinching away.

"Oh, stop it," he snapped out at her. "It's a fucking mug; It's not like I slapped you!"

"You scared me!" she cried.

"Scared you?" he snapped. "Now you're scared of me?"

"You tried to fucking rape me, Steven!" Ivy screamed at him.

"RAPE YOU?" he shouted. "If I had wanted to rape you, I could have."

"Is that supposed to make me feel better?" she cried.

"You're not who I thought you were," he said, not looking at her.

"I'm not who I thought I was either."

Steven's fists clenched. "You betrayed me."

Ivy's heart banged and her head went hot. "I betrayed you?" she said. "You're really... YOU, Steven Rhodes, are accusing ME of betraying YOU?"

"I don't know who you are," he said. "Not anymore."

"I know that now," she said. "And I should have realised that a long time ago. Do you know something, Steven, I HATE blueberry muffins. I hate other people ordering for me like I'm a child. I hate you forcing yourself on me and thinking that's something I could ever want! I hate what I was turning into being with you - some meek, subservient person. I hate that I let you. I'm not that person and I'm never going to be that person again! I'm going to do my Masters; I'm going to get my job. I'm going to be independent and free and far away from you! And THAT is what will make me happy."

Steven looked her up and down with disgust, turned away and walked out of the house, slamming the door behind him, leaving Ivy panting in the kitchen, then falling onto the floor in tears.

Chapter Nineteen

When Ivy's mother and father arrived at Steven's apartment, Ivy opened the front door surrounded by suitcases. It hadn't taken her long to pack. She'd stopped unpacking long ago; her ornaments and pictures and books were mostly still in boxes. Half her clothes were still in suitcases. She'd never felt at home enough to spread as she normally would.

"Ivy?" asked her mother, staring at the suitcases and her tear-stained face.

"Can I come back home, please?"

"Oh, baby!" Emmeline pulled Ivy into her arms.

Ivy cried into her mother's shoulder as her father stroked her hair tenderly.

Back at her parents', she looked at the chintzy duvet cover, the McFly poster, the exercise bike draped in laundry. This wasn't her home, but it was *a* home. More than Steven's had ever been.

Her phone was buzzing away in her pocket - offers of murder from Mya, offers of residence from Julia. She put the phone down, sat on the bed, and took a deep breath.

She didn't need to cry anymore.

***

The exam was hard but being away from Steven had given her extra time and energy to focus on revision. She studied at work on her breaks, poring over her notes while Ben brought her coffee to fuel her efforts, and when she came home, she studied more. When she handed in her exam paper, she felt butterflies but a funny sense of contentment. She knew whatever mark she received it was right. She had done everything she could, for better or worse.

Two weeks before Christmas she got her results.

"How'd you do?" asked Ben as soon as she stepped into the restaurant, twenty minutes before her shift, on the morning after her results came out.

"Nailed it," she said, grinning.

"I knew it," he said, smiling at her, and held out his hand. When she took it, he gave her a little bow as he shook it formally. She laughed. "Congratulations, Ms Rhodes."

"Thank you, Mr Cope," she said, giving a curtsy.

"A coffee?" he offered her, as their hands parted.

"Thank you," she said, slipping into a bar stool two down from where he had been working. Her usual spot.

"And how about a celebratory muffin?" he offered her. "Apricot right?"

"Thank you," she said. "That's perfect."

He served her with a flourish before sitting back down. "So, no more school until the new year?" he asked.

"That's right," she said, picking a bit off her muffin and eating it. "Free 'til January."

"Good," he said. "We're booked up until after new year now. I'm afraid it means you won't get much free time."

Ivy shrugged. "I like to be busy," she said. "And I like being here."

"I like you being here," he said.

Ivy blinked then looked at her coffee. Ben coughed awkwardly then started gathering up his things in a hurry. "Well, better get back there and get on with some proper work before uncle Mal catches me," he said. "See you later."

Ivy watched as he hurried away. She picked at her muffin and sipped her coffee, pondering.

At the end of the day, she headed back to her parents' house. Her father greeted her from where he was cooking a large roast chicken in the oven with roast potatoes and lots of veg.

"Evening, Dad," she said.

"Hello love," he said, smiling at her as he poked the chicken with a metal prodder. "Want me to get you a glass of wine?"

"Don't worry, I'll get it," she said, hanging her coat up and heading to the fridge.

"Good day?" he asked.

Ivy nodded as she poured out the wine. It had been a good day, but her head was whizzing with thoughts. Complicated thoughts she hadn't really had an opportunity to indulge in exploring yet.

"I got some of those sausages without meat in for you," he said, clinking his wine glass on hers. "I'm practising my Christmas day vegetables."

"You need to practise vegetables?" she asked.

"Of course," he said. "I don't really understand why, but your mother cares a lot about the Christmas day vegetables. I don't know what that husband of yours was like, young Ivy, but find yourself a man who will care about what you care about, even if he doesn't understand why you care."

Ivy smiled at her father and kissed his cheek. "I love you, Dad."

Her father got awkward and went back to stirring his carrots.

"Do you need help, or can I go take a shower?"

"You crack on, pet," he said. "I'll give you a shout when your mum gets home."

Ivy headed upstairs with her wine and sat on the bed. She had a lot to think about.

***

Just as Ben had predicted, the restaurant was very busy over Christmas. Ivy worked late on Christmas Eve and started early on Christmas Day. She was rushed off her feet, and absolutely exhausted, but happier than she had been in a long time.

"Hey Ivy," said Ben as she was leaving on Christmas Day, when all the tables had been cleaned and all the lights turned off. "Wait up."

"You okay?" she asked him as he hurried over.

"I just wanted to give you a Christmas gift," he said, holding out a small parcel wrapped in silver.

"Oh!" Ivy exclaimed. "I didn't know we were doing this... I didn't get you anything!"

"That's okay," he insisted. "I didn't expect anything back. And it's not big anyway."

Ivy held it in her hands and smiled for a moment. "Thank you," she said.

"Merry Christmas, Ivy," he said. "Have a good evening."

"You too," she said.

When she got home, she crashed on the sofa to watch the Strictly Come Dancing special with her parents, then eat the dinner her father had been rehearsing. She noted that the vegetables were excellent, and he beamed with pride.

Her parents had put off opening any gifts until Ivy got home, so after dinner they sat around with a bottle of brandy and had a lovely drunken time opening everything up. Mya had given her a silver necklace with a star on, and Julia, a designer handbag.

When she had opened everything else, Ivy took the little silver parcel from her handbag.

"Who's that from?" asked her mum, sloshing some more brandy into Ivy's glass.

"Ben. At work."

"Oh, aye," said her father giving Ivy's mother a look.

Pulling off the wrapping paper, she found a set of beautiful Rotring radiograph pens and cartridges, the kind she used for technical drawings at college, but much nicer than the ones she had now.

"Wow," she said. "That's so kind."

Ivy's mother picked up the pens and examined them. "How did he know you use these?"

"I guess he did some research," she said quietly, holding the box of pens in her hands.

**

In January, things eased up at the restaurant that Ivy was able to focus on finding herself somewhere to live. She was ready.

After some research, and she found a little apartment available that seemed to fit her needs. It was located a comfortable distance between the restaurant and college, on a bus route, and with a low enough rent that she wouldn't have to choose between food and rent. At least, not all the time.

Keen to see her daughter in a home she deemed adequate, and not quite being emotionally ready for Ivy to move out again, Emmeline went with her to meet the lettings agent, Sarah, at 3A Clifford Street.

Walking from the car, Emmeline looked around suspiciously. "It's a bit... rough," she muttered.

Ivy knew it wasn't the sort of area her mother would want her to live, with its run-down shops and shabby-looking pubs, but Ivy didn't care.

When Sarah opened the door onto the little studio apartment in the basement of the building, Emmeline stepped in and looked around, wrinkling her nose.

"Oh, boy," her mother muttered.

Ivy looked around. Old fashioned, but clean, with everything she needed. There was a small bathroom to the left, a kitchenette under the basement window, and a sofa bed at the back. There was room for a little table to work, a bookcase, and a rail for at least some of her clothes. It wasn't much, but it was everything she needed right now.

"It's perfect," said Ivy, nodding, satisfied.

"Seriously?" gasped her mother.

"I know it's a little dated," said Sarah hurriedly. "But that's why the rent is so low."

"A LITTLE dated?" said Emmeline.

"Mum," said Ivy. "This isn't for you. It's for me."

"And the landlord is fine with you decorating," Sarah went on. "As long as it's tasteful."

"That's great," said Ivy. "I'll take it."

"Ivy, darling," said her mother, putting a hand on Ivy's arm. "Why don't you just stay at home?"

"No, Mum" said Ivy.

"Or, we could help you!" her mother went on, then turned to Sarah. "You'd be able to find her a better place if we gave her, say, a few hundred a month towards rent?"

"Well, yes," said Sarah. "Of course."

"No, thank you, Mum," said Ivy.

She understood, but she didn't want it. The flat was small, but she could cook, she could sleep, she could work. She could get to her job and her classes. Right now, that was all she needed from a home.

Plus, most importantly, it wasn't imprinted with anybody else's life. It was a cosy little blank slate. Just hers.

She had been beholden to other people her entire life, lived with roommates, family, friends, and Steven. She had never lived alone, never been entirely responsible for herself. Never figured out how to do it, how to exist and live without support, without people making decisions for her. She had been too scared to even try for so long, and, if she was honest with herself, that was the main reason she'd decided to try giving her marriage another go. But not anymore. Accepting her mother's money might get her a bigger flat, but it would take away some of the independence she had come to realise she needed.

She knew what she wanted now, and she knew how to get it.

"But Ivy, darling," her mother pleaded.

"Mum, it's fine. It's warm, it's clean. It's safe. I'm a grown up, and it's time I started acting like one. This is where I can afford, so this is where I will live."

"But you have us!" her mother insisted. "You don't have to live here."

Ivy gave her mother a hug. "Yes, Mum, I do," she said. "And I want to."

Her mother nodded, accepting. "Very well," she said with a shrug.

Ivy turned to Sarah. "I'll take it," she said again.

The next week, Ivy moved everything she needed into the little apartment. As well as her essential clothes and books, work things and kitchen tools, she had brought the little matchstick house. She had nowhere to put it, but it didn't feel right to leave it.

Wrapping the matchbox house in tissue, she put it in a shoe box under her bed. It deserved a home that she couldn't give it, but at least it was still loved.

She set about painting the walls a soft, pale yellow, and arranged her books on a cheap bookcase she'd found in a charity shop. Her parents bought her a housewarming gift of a brand-new kettle and a supermarket delivery.

College started up again, and she found the balance between work and lessons easier to manage than ever before. She ate when she wanted, what she wanted, and she slept comfortably. Her little apartment became a truly special place for her. Just hers.

Whenever she could, she took extra shifts at the restaurant, covering other people's jobs as well as her own, and was always busy. Partly because she needed the money, and partly because she felt very happy in that space.

One Monday morning, she was working behind the bar with Ben when they saw Malcolm come in. Ivy was surprised. The restaurant was quiet and he'd taken the week off to have a post-Christmas rush break.

"Uncle Mal," said Ben, sounding as surprised as Ivy felt. "I wasn't expecting you in this week."

"Are you here for a drink?" asked Ivy.

"I'm here for my second in command," said Malcolm, pointing at Ben. "I expected to find you in the office."

"Trev called in sick," said Ben. "So, I'm covering the bar right now."

"I see that," said Malcolm, resting his elbows on the bar and looking around. There was a couple of people dotted around the restaurant, but it was mostly quiet. "Tell me, Benjamin, is there any reason two of you are needed to work the bar when Trev usually handles a quiet Monday like this alone?"

Ben's mouth opened and closed for a moment, his cheeks flushing. "Well, erm, you see..."

Malcolm stood up straight again and gave Ben a look. "I thought as much." He turned to Ivy. "Say hello to your father for me?"

"Of course," said Ivy, her cheeks burning.

"Tell him I'll be in touch to sort out a game of squash again soon?"

"I'll do that," said Ivy, nodding.

"And Ben?"

"Yes?"

"I appreciate your efforts to keep our staff happy, but we have a business to run too. Don't forget that."

"Yes Uncle Mal,"

Malcolm smiled warmly at Ivy then gave Ben another look, then headed back out of the restaurant.

Ben turned to Ivy, looking embarrassed. "I get bored when I'm covering it alone," he said. "And I figured you'd appreciate the break from the scales..."

"Oh, definitely," said Ivy. "And Tia's good up front. She likes it. The wig suits her."

"Yeah, exactly," said Ben. "So, it just made sense really."

"Yeah," said Ivy. "It makes sense."

Ben smiled and got back to polishing glasses.

***

Winter turned to spring. Her parents regularly came round, her father often smuggling in things that he'd taken out of her bedroom at their house to try and clear space, and her mother rolling her eyes and taking them away again with a reassuring pat on Ivy's arm.

She saw Mya and Julia occasionally, but not as often as before, because she was working so many hours and preparing for her final exams. But they kept in touch and saw each other for catchups when they could. But mostly her life was work, then school, then work, then school.

When the week of her final exams came around, she was stressed out of her mind. She studied constantly, practised drawings with her new pens from Ben, and struggled to sleep. This was her chance. If she did well in these, she could finally get onto the Masters course. Nearly ten years late, admittedly, but still. Better late than never.

Gloria Clarke was encouraging, Olivia, who she often did project work with, was confident. But Ivy was terrified. What if, after everything, she fucked it all up now.

"You've got this," said Ben, catching her studying a book under the podium when she was working one afternoon.

"Sorry," she said, closing the book. "It's just, it's quiet and, I've not got long left to get this into my head."

"It's fine," he said, putting a hand on her arm for a second. "Do what you've got to do. But trust me, you're the smartest person I've ever met. You've got this."

"Thank you," she said.

The morning of her last exam, her phone lit up repeatedly, flashing with messages of good luck and love from her friends and parents. She held it tightly before turning it off and heading into the exam room.

It was now or never. She was either going to get what she had worked for and wanted so desperately, or lose it all. She sat in her seat, picked up her pen, and took a deep breath. She was ready.

A couple of months later, Ivy was in the kitchenette of her little flat on Clifford Street getting wine glasses out of the cupboard when she heard a knock on the front door.

As she pulled it open, she was immediately coated in party popper streamers as Mya and Julia shouted "CONGRATULATIONS!" at her.

Ivy laughed, brushing the streamers off herself and stepped back to let them in.

"Hi!"

"Ivy, we've missed you!" yelled Mya, throwing her arms around her.

"You look different," said Julia, looking Ivy up and down before hugging her too.

"I feel different," said Ivy. "I feel better."

"Do you feel like your brain is heavier now?" asked Mya.

Ivy got wine from the fridge and poured it into the wine glasses, grinning at her friends. "Definitely. Can barely hold my head up."

"This place looks great," said Julia, accepting the glass of wine Ivy handed to her. "It's very homely."

Ivy smiled. Julia, coming from her elegant and grown-up space full of chic artwork and expensive furniture, was complimenting her little basement apartment with no room for a proper sofa. And the thing was, she genuinely meant it. Julia was like that.

"Thanks," she said. "I'm really happy here. But I forgot about food. I only got home from the restaurant fifteen minutes ago, I'm so sorry."

"I'll order a pizza," said Mya, getting her phone out and going onto the app.

"So," said Julia, leaning against the counter. "Tell us EVERYTHING. I feel like we've not spoken to you in years."

"I know," said Ivy. "But it'll calm down a bit now school's finished."

"When's your graduation?" Mya asked as she tapped on the phone screen.

"The third of next month," she said. "I've got to get my gown and cap sorted."

"Eeeek!" squealed Mya.

"I know," said Ivy. "About time too, right?"

"Damn bloody right." Said Mya.

"When do you start your Masters?" asked Julia.

"In a couple of months," she said. "I've started buying my books."

"Have you made a move on Ben yet?" asked Mya, tucking the phone back in her jeans and sipping innocently on the glass of wine.

Ivy snorted. "No!"

"Oh my god, Ivy," groaned Mya. "What are you doing? You're killing me."

"I'm not ready yet," she said, shrugging and sipping her wine. "I've got enough to focus on without thinking about sex."

"I didn't say sex," said Mya, with a mischievous grin. "That was all you, babe."

Mya and Julia exchanged a grin.

"It's good to see you happy," said Julia.

"Julia's happy too," said Mya. "She got a promotion."

"You did?" asked Ivy.

"Yeah," said Julia. "Director of Sales and Marketing."

"Oh my god!" cried Ivy, jumping up and hugging her friend. "I'm so happy for you!"

"Stonking great raise too," said Mya, raising her glass.

"Shh," said Julia, flapping a hand at Mya.

"That's absolutely brilliant, Julia," said Ivy. "I can't believe you didn't tell me though!"

"You've been busy," said Julia, shrugging. "I didn't want to burden you."

"Oh, Julia," she said, feeling like the worst friend in the world. "I'm so sorry. I've been so busy. I really do care about your lives, you know."

"I know, don't worry. We understand. But, whilst we're on the subject, Mya has news too," said Julia, elbowing Mya.

"What?" asked Ivy.

"I... met someone," said Mya, suddenly going shy.

"A real someone?" gasped Ivy, and Julia choked on her wine with laughter.

"No, a shop window mannequin," said Mya, rolling her eyes. "Yes, a real someone, you idiot."

"Who?" cried Ivy.

"Her name's Connie," said Mya, looking all dreamy-eyed in a way Ivy had never seen before. "She's in costume design, so her department's always working with mine, and she's... she's just so incredible."

"Mya!" cried Ivy. "Look at you! You're all mushy!"

"Oh shush," Mya said. "But yeah. I am. I'm mushy."

"That's wonderful," said Ivy, putting a hand on Mya's arm. "I'm so happy for you."

"A toast to Mya's mush!" said Julia, holding up her glass.

"Mya's mush!" said Ivy and they clinked glasses as Mya cracked up laughing.

"I've missed you," said Mya, wiping tears of laughter from her eyes.

"I've missed you too," said Ivy. "I can't believe how much I've missed!"

"Life gets in the way sometimes," said Julia. "We're catching up now."

Ivy shook her head, realising how little time she'd given to her friends recently. It wasn't fair. She'd put so much time into school and work that she'd forgotten them a bit and it wasn't good. She determined to find a better balance.

The pizza arrived and they settled into drinking and eating and chatting as if they'd never been apart at all. But they had. And moving on with her life didn't mean moving on without the people that mattered the most in it.

Except for one. Mya and Julia had moved on with their lives. She needed to move on with hers too.

The next day she phoned a lawyer and booked an appointment.

Chapter Twenty

Ivy carefully adjusted her cap and smoothed out her robes before posing for photos with her parents underneath a picture-book tree in the college grounds.

"Stop crying, Mum!" Ivy said laughing, "you're smudging your mascara."

"I can't help it," said Emmeline, taking a tissue out of her bra and dabbing her cheeks with it. "I always dreamed this day would come."

"Eventually," said Ivy.

"Better late than never," said her father, sniffing.

"Dad! You didn't even cry at my wedding."

"Well obviously," he said, straightening up and looking serious. "That was happenstance. But this? This is accomplishment."

Ivy gave her father a hug, and over his shoulder saw Steven skulking by some trees. Watching.

She froze. What did he want? What was she supposed to do?

"Are you alright?" asked her father, as Ivy stiffly stood back from him.

"Ivy, darling?" asked her mum, trying to see what had caught Ivy's attention, but Steven had obviously ducked out of sight.

Ivy got herself together. "I'll just be back in a minute, okay?"

"Okay, sweetheart," said her mum as Ivy marched across the garden to where she had spotted him lurking.

She saw him, standing nervously behind a plum tree, dressed in a suit as if he was an invited guest there to celebrate, not a wanker ruining her perfect day.

"What are you doing here?" she demanded.

"I wanted to congratulate you," he said.

"Thank you," she said. *Bullshit.* "What do you really want?"

"You're doing the Masters?" he asked her, ignoring the question.

"Yes," she said. "I got accepted."

"That's great," he said. "I'm really proud of you."

"What do you want, Steven?" she asked. She looked over her shoulder and saw her parents watching her. Could they see Steven skulking in the shadows? "I've got stuff to do. We're celebrating."

"My lawyer called," he said. "You filed for divorce."

"Yes," she said, "I did."

He looked at her; he looked in pain. He looked hurt. "Why?" he asked her.

"What do you mean why? That's what happens when a marriage ends," she said. "You get divorced. What did you think was going to happen?"

"But..."

"Come on, Steven," she said. *Don't do this. Don't make this day about you.* "You must have expected this."

"We could talk," he said, reaching out to try and touch her. She stepped back. She never wanted him to touch her again.

"No," she said. "We talked. We both know how that went."

"Ivy, come on," he pleaded. She looked at him; he looked almost pitiful. She hesitated. He took the opportunity to reach out again and grab her hand. He held it tightly, rubbing the bare ring finger with his thumb. "We've been married for nearly six years! That's real. That matters. You know it does."

"You don't want me, Steven," she said, taking her hand back. "Not really. You want your image of me, your ideal version of me. But not me."

"I love you, Ivy," he said, pleading with her.

"Steven..."

"Please, Ivy, I hate being alone. I miss you. Come home with me, Ivy. Come home."

"I have a home," she said. Enough. He wasn't going to waste any more of her time. "Sign the papers, Steven."

"Ivy..."

"I've got to go," she said, stepping away from him. "I've got some celebrating to do."

Ivy walked away from him and didn't look back. Together with her parents, she headed to The Seven Seas Restaurant where they met Mya, Julia and Fred (Mya said it was a bit early to throw Connie at the entire family), and Ben and Malcolm threw them a party to celebrate her graduation.

Malcolm popped a bottle of champagne and everybody cheered. Ivy's mother cried. Ivy's father pretended he wasn't crying. Malcolm joined them both and sobbed openly.

"It's like when my little girl graduated," he said, sniffing heavily as he handed them champagne.

Ivy laughed with joy to see them so proud and happy, then turned and saw Ben walking towards her, beaming.

"You look wonderful," he said, handing her a glass of champagne.

Ivy smiled at him. He looked wonderful too, she thought.

Malcolm came over and gave Ivy a hug. "Oh Ivy," he said. "You are a star. My Seren graduated years ago now, but it's still one of the proudest days of my life."

"That's lovely," said Ivy.

He wiped a tear from his eye, then glanced at his nephew with a mischievous look on his face.

"I hope young Ben here is taking care of you?" he asked.

"He is," she said. "Thank you."

"Good, good. Perhaps one day he'll take you out and buy you a drink himself," said Malcolm. "Instead of just giving out my stuff for free."

"Uncle Mal!" said Ben, looking mortified.

Malcolm held his hands up in mock innocence and Ivy tried to hide her smile, then he gave her another hug and headed back to join her parents.

Ivy glanced at Ben shyly.

"So, what's next?" he asked her.

Ivy shrugged. "I've got a summer of friends and family and work before I get back to studying," she said.

"So, you'll have some free time?" he asked her.

"Yeah," she said. "Some."

"Cool," he said, sipping his drink. "Cool."

Mya and Julia headed over and clinked glasses with Ivy. "Is this not the most glorious woman you've ever seen in your life?" asked Mya, putting an arm around Ivy.

"Definitely," said Ben, laughing.

Mya and Julia exchanged a look. Ivy was very used to seeing that look.

***

Standing in her old bedroom at her mum and dad's house, Ivy sorted through her belongings. She had several

full boxes to take to the charity shop, a couple of bin bags
of things to throw out, and only a couple of bags of things
to keep.

She opened her suitcase, the one she'd taken to Steven's
house and had never felt like using again. Inside was the
grey and black scarf.

Her mother opened the door and came in, handing her a
cup of coffee. "How's it going?"

"Good, actually," she said. "Dad can stop moaning
about my clutter now."

"He'll find something else to moan about," she said with
a shrug. "It's part of his grumpy old bugger persona. He's
quite sweet behind all that."

Ivy smiled. "Yeah, I've noticed that."

She picked up the scarf and moved it about in her
fingers, then carefully folded it up and put it into a
donations box.

"You're not keeping much," said her mother, watching
her.

"No," she said. "I don't need to anymore."

Emmeline gave Ivy a gentle rub on the arm then left her
to it.

That night, Ivy headed to The Seven Seas restaurant.

"Hey there," said Daisy who was standing at the
podium and sporting the water nymph costume, looking
pretty pleased about it. "Your friends are already here."

"Great, thanks," said Ivy. She hurried through to the bar
where Mya and Julia were sitting at a table next to a fish
tank, with cocktails.

"Sorry," she said. "I got held up at my mum's."

They both greeted her with cheek kisses, and she sat
down. Trev came to the table.

"Drink, Ivy?"

"Pinot?" she asked.

"Coming right up," he said.

"So," said Julia, trying to look innocent and failing. "How come you wanted to meet here?"

"On your night off?" added Mya.

"No reason," said Ivy. "It's close to home is all."

"Ah," said Julia with a knowing smile. "Of course, convenience."

"Say," said Mya. "Is Ben working tonight?"

"Maybe," said Ivy, and letting her gaze wander around the restaurant. Because of course that was why she'd chosen there. She knew it, they knew it, but she'd be damned if she straight up confessed it. "I dunno."

It had been a whole week since Ben had vaguely hinted at possibly spending time together at Ivy's graduation celebration. A whole week since the suggestion of him taking her out had been made. A whole week of shy, furtive glances across the restaurant towards one another. A whole week of conversations starting before being interrupted by a customer or colleague. A whole week of text chats about films and TV and books, jokes exchanged, and goodnight messages from bed every night, and good morning messages the next day.

A whole week.

"You're so full of crap!" Julia laughed.

Trev returned with her wine and set it down. Ivy took a grateful swig. She felt incredibly nervous but absolutely ridiculous for it.

"How long 'til Connie gets here?" she asked after swallowing the alcohol.

Mya suddenly straightened up and a huge smile broke out across her face. "She's right here!"

Ivy turned and saw a tall woman with blonde hair walking towards them, with a matching smile, her eyes locked onto Mya. Mya got out of her chair and greeted her with a hug and a gentle kiss, before turning back to Ivy and Julia.

"Connie, these are my friends, Ivy and Julia," she said, her hand finding Connie's and holding it tight. "Guys, this is Connie."

"It's so great to meet you," said Connie warmly. "Mya's told me so much about you."

"She's been pretty non-stop about you, too," said Julia, winking at Mya.

Connie and Mya slipped into seats at the table and Connie looked thrilled, leaning into Mya affectionately, while Mya looked like she was suddenly glowing.

"This place is so cute," said Connie, looking around. "This is where you work, right, Ivy?"

"Yeah, that's right. I'm usually in the green wig up front," she said.

"Amazing! I worked on a show about mermaids once," she said. "It got cancelled pretty fast, but it was great fun while it lasted."

"You're a costume designer, right?" said Ivy.

"Yeah, that's right," she said, smiling. "I'll go get us some drinks; do you guys need another?"

"No, we're good, thanks," said Julia.

"Cool, I'll be right back," said Connie, standing up.

"I'll come with you," said Mya.

Connie and Mya headed to the bar to order and Ivy smiled at Julia. Neither of them had seen Mya so contented with another human, in all the years they'd known her. It was beautiful. Ivy let herself feel jealous for a moment then pushed it away. It wasn't about her failures in love, it was about Mya finding such success.

"Hey," came a voice behind her. Ivy startled and watched as Julia's face spread into an even bigger smile.

She turned and saw Ben standing next to her, smiling. "Ben!" she said. "Hello! Hi!"

Oh god, calm down. You sound ridiculous.

"I didn't know you were coming in tonight," he said.

"I just thought that it was a good place to come, and we're meeting Mya's new girlfriend, so I thought this was a fun place, and everybody likes it here, and I like it here, I mean, I like being here, and I..." Julia kicked her sharply under the table. "OUCH!"

"Are you okay?" Ben asked.

"Grand!" said Ivy. Julia rolled her eyes.

Mya and Connie arrived back from the bar carrying cocktails.

"Hey! What a surprise to see you here!" said Mya, tilting her head and giving Ivy a look.

"Hey, Mya, said Ben, then he held a hand out to Connie. "We've not met. I'm Ben."

She shook his offered hand. "Connie," she said. "I'm Mya's girlfriend."

Ivy wondered if Ben would react. Men usually reacted.

"Are you guys being looked after?" he asked them. Not a blink.

"We are," said Julia. "Thanks."

"Fab. That's great. Erm, Ivy," he said, suddenly looking nervous. "I was wondering..."

The three women observing them suddenly became incredibly fixated on their menus.

"Yes?"

"I'm finishing in a few minutes," he said. "Would I be able to buy you a drink? As in, actually *buy* one for you, not just give you a freebie on Uncle Mal, 'cause you're a co-worker..."

Oh god! Now?? Now!? Ivy's gut churned. *YES! But not now!* Not when she'd made a vow to stop being so self-absorbed and start being a better friend.

"That'd be lovely," said Ivy. "Really, it would. But it's a bit of a girl's night tonight..."

Ivy saw Julia look up suddenly with a glare. Mya rapidly shook her head at her. But Ivy ignored them. She'd made a promise. Good friend.

"Oh, totally!" said Ben. "Of course. Maybe another night?"

Yay!

"Friday night?" she suggested, hopefully.

Ben went from looking dejected, but stoical, to jubilant in a split second. "Friday night would be perfect," he said. "Somewhere else?"

"Verso?" she suggested. "At eight?"

Ben nodded, sighing with relief and pleasure, then smiled at her again. "Verso at eight," he said. "I'll be there. Okay. Great. Good. Excellent. Yes. Well. Right. I'll be off then. I'll have a word and make sure you get the celebrity treatment tonight. Not that we ever get celebrities here, I mean, I just..." Ben started to look horrified. Ivy had never seen him so flustered.

"Thanks," said Julia, cutting in and offering him a supportive smile. "We appreciate it."

"Welcome," he said, nodding. "See you soon, Ivy."

Ben hurried away and Julia turned towards Ivy with furious exasperation. "What are you thinking?" she cried.

"You could have had a drink with him now! We'd have understood!"

Ivy shrugged. "I can wait," she said. "Tonight is for you guys."

Julia put a hand on Ivy's and squeezed. "If you're sure."

"Absolutely," she said.

She knew what she wanted.

"Come on," said Mya. "Let's order. I'm starving."

***

Ben was waiting for her when she got there. Collar open, shirt sleeves rolled up so she could see the jigsaw puzzle tattoo, and a broad smile on his face as he saw her approach.

He stood up as she reached the table and stepped out.

"You look beautiful," he said, and leaned in to kiss her hesitantly on the cheek. His skin like a soft, warm sandpaper against her cheek. He smelled like fresh linen.

As he stepped back she felt her cheek burning where his skin had been. Her hands were sweating. *Oh shit.* She was in trouble.

"Thank you," she said, her voice croaky and her throat dry.

They sat down and a waitress appeared. "Are you ready to order a drink now?" she asked Ben.

He'd waited for her.

"Do you know what you want?" he asked Ivy. "Or do you want a minute?"

"No, I'm ready," she said. "A glass of Pinot, please."

"A bottle, and we'll share?" he asked.

"That's great," said Ivy.

He turned to the waitress, "A bottle of Pinot Grigio, please."

"Coming right up!"

The waitress left and Ben turned back to her. He shuffled awkwardly on his seat.

"So," he said. "I'm going to make a confession."

"Yeah?"

"I'm really nervous."

Ivy smiled. "Me too."

"I feel like we've never had a conversation before," he said, shaking his head. "I know that's daft. We talk every day."

Ivy laughed. "I know what you mean though! This is... this is different."

The waitress came back with the wine, poured it into two glasses and left again. Ben's eyes stayed on Ivy's, a nervous smile on his lips.

He held up his glass to Ivy, and she mirrored him. They clinked. "Here's to making it worth the wait."

Ivy smiled. "Worth the wait."

They spent the evening talking and laughing, eating and drinking. Soon the nerves had fallen away, and they fell into their normal pattern of chatting and laughing. It was the same, but different.

At the end of the night, Ben saw her into a taxi with a second kiss on the cheek, and Ivy headed home feeling just a tiny bit drunk and very happy. By the time she got to her little flat, she had a text from Ben thanking her for a lovely evening, hoping for a second date, and with the goodnight that she had grown accustomed to receiving from him.

Ivy sat on the edge of her sofa bed, took off her shoes, and laughed. Yes, she was ready. She was finally ready.

As the summer moved on, she worked at the restaurant, she spent time with her friends, and she had dinners with her parents. She prepared for starting her Masters by studying hard and she felt like she was doing the things she was always supposed to do with her life. And, when she wasn't doing all of those things, she saw Ben. She saw Ben at the cinema; she saw Ben in the pub; she saw Ben in her bed.

By the time September came around, everyone knew she and Ben were together and Uncle Mal was so delighted he spent more and more time in the restaurant, just so he could be around them. She was introduced to the wonderful Seren, who truly was everything her father had promised: a philosophy teacher with a passion and talent for tap dancing. She was funny, smart and capable of holding her liquor. Ben loved his cousin dearly, and she and Ivy soon became firm friends.

One evening, Ivy nervously introduced her new friend Seren, to her old friends Mya and Julia. They hit it off immediately and soon an evening for Mya, Connie, Julia, Fred, Seren, her husband, Lucas, Ivy and Ben was arranged.

Lucas owned a roofing business, and he and Fred had immediately bonded over Liverpool FC. Connie had trained as a dancer before moving into costume design, so she and Seren talked about tap dancing and stage performances. Ivy found her social circle grew to accommodate her relationship in a way it never had with Steven. Her girls' nights still happened but started to be replaced by the entire circle getting together.

The first week of her Masters was intense, but Ivy had never been happier. She felt like she was finally starting her real life.

Chapter Twenty-One

"Ivy," said her mother, examining her. "You look tired."

"Final weeks," she said, sitting down opposite her mother in Verso. "So yeah, I'm tired."

Emmeline tutted. "Are you looking after yourself?"

"Yes mother," she said with a laugh. "I'm thirty-four years old. You really don't have to worry."

"I will always worry," she said, smiling. "It's my job."

"I know," said Ivy.

"How's Ben?"

"He's fabulous," she said. "He sends his love."

Emmeline put a hand to her chest. "How lovely," she said. "When are you coming round again?"

"Soon," she said. "I promise. But with him renovating the new restaurant and me non-stop with uni and work, we're so busy."

"Well as long as you don't forget about your poor old mother," said Emmeline, sipping her wine.

"How could anybody forget you, Mum?"

"Good point," she said. "I'm wonderful."

"I'm sorry I've been so caught up in everything," said Ivy. "I promise it's not forever. We're so close to getting everything we ever wanted. We just have to push through this last stage."

"I know," said Emmeline "I'm whinging, but honestly my darling, we are so proud of you."

"Thanks, Mum" said Ivy, smiling.

***

Ivy's final weeks of her Masters, full of exams and presentations, went by so fast she could hardly believe it.

This thing that she had dreamed of, cried over, longed for... and it was done.

Heading out into the street at the end of her last day at university, Ivy stared up at the building she had grown to treasure. She felt so strange. She had interviews coming up, glowing references from her lecturers, and connections made with industry professionals who were all keen to speak to her. Somehow, without even noticing it, Ivy had become what she always dreamed she could.

Walking down the street, ready to go and join Ben at the restaurant, Ivy spotted someone walking towards her who she thought recognised. She squinted, searching her memories.

Steven.

"Ivy!" he said, spotting her and throwing his arms open. He looked thrilled.

"Hi, Steven," she said. "How are you?"

"I'm great, great," he said. "You know, busy as always. How about you? Busy? How's the job going? Did you ever do that Masters?"

"I'm good," she said. "Look, sorry, Steven, I've got to hurry but it was great to see you."

Ivy gave him a polite wave and moved on. Behind her she heard him call out to her, but she didn't stop. She didn't need to.

When she got to the restaurant, she found Ben, surrounded by ladders and dust sheets, with a bottle of champagne, a lemon cheesecake, and a huge bunch of roses. He had paint on his cheeks and what looked like a poorly applied bandage on his hand from god knows what injury.

"Congratulations!" he cried as she entered.

She laughed and ran to him, throwing her arms around him and kissing him hard. He held her close.

"I love you, Ivy," he said. "And I'm so proud of you."

"I love you too," she said. "Especially considering this."

She pointed to the display he'd set up balanced on a toolbox.

"Well, only the finest gifts for the finest architect," he said.

He popped the cork from the champagne and poured it into two plastic glasses.

"To you," he said, handing hers to her.

"To me," she said, smiling happily and sipping her drink.

"We'll be ready for the electrics to be finished soon," he said, looking around. "Final fixtures."

"Amazing," she said. "It's looking great in here."

"Be weird to work around people who aren't dressed like fish," he said. "Do you think you'll miss it?"

"The fish costumes? No," she said. "The people though."

"They're a good lot," he said. "And we'll still see them. Uncle Mal will hit the roof if we don't come by at least once a week."

Ivy laughed and rested a cheek on his shoulder.

"That place was special to me," she said. "I feel like starting work there changed my life. I dunno where I'd be today if he hadn't offered me that job."

"Remind me to buy him a pint soon," said Ben. "Because an alternative reality where you're not here doesn't bear thinking about."

Ivy kissed him. It really didn't.

"Don't forget it's Mya's engagement party later," she said after a moment. "Will you be ready?"

"Definitely not," he said, "But I'll be there anyway."

"Good," she said. "Now let's eat this cheesecake, because it's staring at me and I need to destroy it with my face."

He handed her a fork.

***

"Ivy! Ben!" cried Mya, falling on them when they arrived at Verso later that night.

"Congratulations, Mya," said Ivy, holding her friend close.

Behind her Connie came over and hugged them both in turn too. "Thanks for coming," she said.

Mya slipped a hand into Connie's and smiled at her.

"You guys look gorgeous," said Ivy. Mya, her emerald green spangly top contrasting beautifully with her shocking purple pixie crop, gave her a twirl.

"There's shots on the bar," said Connie, after taking a moment to admire her fiancée.

"Shots? Oh boy," laughed Ivy.

"Tequila," said Mya. "Your favourite."

Ivy spotted Julia and Fred and headed in their direction with Ben, leaving Mya and Connie to greet more guests.

"Well, if it isn't the qualified architect," said Julia. "And her handsome restaurateur."

Ivy gave a curtsy as Ben shook Fred's hand and kissed Julia's cheek.

"Are you guys in for the shots?" asked Fred.

"When in Rome," said Ivy.

They all took their shot glasses, clinked glasses, and drank them. "Fuck a bloody duck!" gasped Ben. "Strong stuff."

When it was time for speeches, Mya held her glass up high. "I would like you all to raise your glasses to Constance Day," she said. "The most incredible woman I have ever had the pleasure of meeting. The strongest, the kindest, the most intelligent, and the most gorgeous human this planet has to offer. Thank you for loving me, Con."

Connie leaned over and rested her forehead against Mya's as everyone cheered.

"To Connie!" shouted Julia.

"And," Mya went on. "To my best friends in the world. Julia and Ivy. Without you guys I'd never have found her. You two shepherded my drunk ass through uni, followed me around the world and made sure I always got home." She paused, emotions taking over her. She took a second as Connie held her hand tight before Mya looked up towards them again, tears on her cheeks. "And you showed me the importance of love. You loved me no matter what; you loved me for the truth of me. You loved me at my best and at my worst, and you made me believe I deserved it. And then, with all the love you gave me, you taught me to love you right back. The love I have for you guys changed me. It made me a better person, and it made me worthy of this woman. Thank you."

Ivy wiped a tear from her eye as around the room people raised their glasses. Ben smiled at her proudly and clinked his glass against hers.

"You're a life-changing woman," he whispered to her.

When they finally made it back to Ivy's little flat, they fell onto her sofa bed and held one another, drunkenly laughing and full of joy.

"Ivy," he said, stroking her hair gently from her face. "Will you live with me?"

"What?" she asked him.

"Move in with me," he said. "Please. We are about to start our real lives. You're qualified and you're going to be incredible. My restaurant opens soon. I want my real life to start each day seeing you, and end each day in your arms. I can't imagine any other way. Please, live with me."

Ivy felt tears in her eyes, and she leaned over and kissed him. "I will," she said. "I will."

And she did.

Two weeks later, Ivy found herself once again packing her belongings. But this time Ben was there to help.

"What's this?" he asked, taking the shoe box out from under her bed and finding the little matchstick house inside.

"The first house I ever designed," she said, smiling.

"How old were you?" he asked her.

"About six," she said, shrugging. "It's silly. I only keep it because, I dunno..."

"Are you kidding? It's amazing."

He carefully wrapped it back up into the shoe box, then put the shoe box into the packing box. Ivy watched him, her heart full.

When they got to his, they unloaded the van and piled the boxes into his living room. Ben picked up the little box and took out the matchstick house.

He took it over the mantelpiece, moved a sports trophy onto a bookcase, and carefully put the matchstick house in its place. "What do you think?" he asked.

Ivy came over. "Perfect," she said. "You found the perfect spot for it."

Two weeks later, Ben opened The Water Nymph restaurant. The chef's food received rave reviews, and Ivy and her friends all celebrated the night away.

Three weeks after that, Ivy attended her Masters graduation ceremony. In front of her friends, her family, and her Ben, she received her Masters Distinction. Two weeks later, she started her first job at an architecture firm, and was put straight to work on a team designing a new school. She loved it, she was good at it and, at the end of the day, she went home and saw her matchstick house in pride of place in the home she shared with the man who valued her.

"How are you, Ivy?" her mum asked her, one evening in Verso, as she poured a bottle of wine into two glasses.

"You know what?"

"What?"

"I'm really happy, Mum," said Ivy. "I'm really, really happy."

Her mum took her hand and squeezed it. "I know you are, baby."

When she got home, she found Ben asleep in bed. She climbed in next to him and snuggled in close. Sleepily, he turned over and wrapped himself around her, kissing her gently on the mouth before drifting back to sleep.

Ivy smiled to herself. Finally, after all this time, she had everything she'd ever wanted.

Read More
Siren Stories: The Ultimate Bibliography

Lilly Prospero And The Magic Rabbit (The Lilly Prospero Series Book 1)
By J.J. Barnes

Lilly Prospero And The Magic Rabbit is a young adult urban fantasy exploring the corrupting effects of absolute power on a teenage girl. When the unpopular and lonely Lilly Prospero is given a talking pet rabbit, her life begins to change. She is thrust into a world of magic, mystery, and danger, and has to get control of a power she doesn't understand fast to make the difference between life and death. The first in a new series by J.J. Barnes, Lilly Prospero And The Magic Rabbit is a tale full of excitement, sorrow and mystery, as Lilly Prospero shows just how strong a girl can be.

Available in Paperback and for Kindle.

Alana: A Ghost Story
By Jonathan McKinney

Alana is a ghost, trapped in the New York Film Academy dorms, where she died. She has friends, fellow ghosts, with whom she haunts the students living there, passing her time watching whatever TV shows and movies the students watch.

But she is restless. She wants to move on. And when a medium moves into the dorms, Alana gets a nasty shock, which turns her mundane afterlife upside down.

Alana is a light yet moving short story about a miraculous love that travels many years and many miles to save a lost, trapped and hopeless soul.

Available in Paperback and for Kindle.

Emily the Master Enchantress: The First Schildmaids Novel (The Schildmaids Saga Book 1)
By Jonathan McKinney

Hidden, veiled behind the compressed wealth of New York City, is a dank underbelly of exploitation and slavery, which most people never see, or sense, or suffer. A cruel, expanding world.

And when Emily Hayes-Brennan, a proficient enchantress with a good heart and a tendency to overshare, is recruited to the world renowned crime fighters, the Schildmaids, she will find that that cruel world threatens to expand around her, and everyone she cares about.

She will be confronted by conflicts of fate and choice, as she seeks to find her place in the world.

Available in Paperback and for Kindle.

After the Mad Dog in the Fog: An Erotic Schildmaids Novelette
By Jonathan McKinney and J.J. Barnes

Emily Hayes-Brennan wants to get through a simple night out in her home city of New York, introducing her new boyfriend Teo to her friends, so she can get him home and have sex with him for the very first time. But when an obnoxious admirer and old flame shows up, she begins to fear that her plans are going awry.

After the Mad Dog in the Fog is a wild and energetic novelette about love and desire, and about the free joy that comes from prioritising the one you love before all others.

Available in Paperback and for Kindle.

Lilly Prospero And The Mermaid's Curse (The Lilly Prospero Series Book 2)
By J.J. Barnes

Lilly Prospero And The Mermaid's Curse is a young adult, urban fantasy following Lilly Prospero and her friend Saffron Jones on a magical adventure to Whitstable.

Whilst on a family holiday, Lilly and Saffron meet mermaids under attack from a mysterious and violent stranger, work with a powerful coven of witches, and fight to save not only the lives of the mermaids, but their own lives as well.

Available in Paperback and for Kindle.

The Inadequacy of Alice Anders: A Schildmaids Short Story
By Jonathan McKinney

Alice Anders can summon vision of the future, which guide her heroic friends through heroic acts. Sometimes she'll see vulnerable people in danger; sometimes she'll see her superhero friends in places where they can help those who can't help themselves.

But, for the last three and a half weeks, she's not been able to summon a single vision—and given that she started working for the superhero team of her dreams, the Schildmaids, exactly three and a half weeks ago, she's becoming anxious about her worth. And to figure out why her power has gone away, she'll have to push herself, and face some hard truths.

The Inadequacy of Alice Anders is a light and bittersweet short story about the pain of loss, and about facing that pain when it threatens to hold you down and hold you back.

Available in Paperback and for Kindle.

The Fundamental Miri Mnene: The Second Schildmaids Novel (The Schildmaids Saga Book 2)
By Jonathan McKinney

Miri Mnene is the Syncerus, a warrior, and the strongest of the Schildmaids, the New York team of legendary crime fighters. But she was not always the Syncerus. Once, she was the Xuétú Nánrén Shashou, the final student of the man-hating, man-killing Guan-yin Cheh.

And when she is sent to South Dakota to investigate a mystical brothel, which has been kidnapping women, kidnapping girls, and forcing them to work, she is confronted by the darkness that lives within her when her past and present collide.

The Fundamental Miri Mnene is a powerful novel about the lengths to which you should go, the lengths to which you must go, in order to see justice in the world.

Available in Paperback and for Kindle.

The Relief of Aurelia Kite: A Schildmaids Novella
By Jonathan McKinney

Aurelia Kite is a young New Yorker at Christmas, trapped in an abusive relationship, dreaming of escape. And when her controlling boyfriend Trafford takes on a new job, her path crosses with two highly serious female crime fighters, causing her to make a big decision about what she will and will not tolerate.

The Relief of Aurelia Kite is a harsh novella with a soft centre, about hope in the face of toxic romance, and about the salvation that can be found just by talking to a sympathetic stranger.

Available in Paperback and for Kindle.

Not Even Stars: The Third Schildmaids Novel
By Jonathan McKinney

Teo Roqué is journeying through Europe with Emily Hayes-Brennan, the woman he loves, when ancient hostilities give way to a war between powerful, clandestine organisations. A war which puts the young couple's lives in danger, as well as all those they care about.

And as a new threat emerges, fanning the conflict's flames, Teo and Emily must work together to end the war before it leads to a disaster much, much worse than they'd imagined.

Not Even Stars is an incredibly intense novel about all-consuming love, about awe-inspiring heroism, and about the cost of making the right choice when the fate of the world hangs in the balance.

Available in Paperback and for Kindle.

The Mystery of Ms. Riley: a Schildmaids Novella
By Jonathan McKinney

Alice Anders and Rakesha McKenzie are members of the Schildmaids, the legendary New York crime fighters. And when Alice sees visions of Nina Riley, a young New Yorker carrying a deep, hidden pain, the two heroes fight to determine what has caused that pain, and how to save Ms. Riley from a prison she cannot even see.

The Mystery of Ms. Riley is a harsh yet hopeful story about self-doubt, about ordinary, everyday oppression, and about the kind of love that defies the testimonies of everyone around you.

Available in Paperback and for Kindle.

Unholy Water: A Halloween Novel
By Jonathan McKinney

In the misty Lancashire town of Ecclesburn, kids go missing. But no one talks about it. Everyone knows why, but they don't talk about it. The grown ups smear garlic and holy water over their necks and wrists while walking the dog after dark, but they never say the V word.

And when one of the local pubs is taken over by a group of undead monsters, and a trio of vampire hunters is called to clear them out, a terrible series of events begins to play out, which will change the way Ecclesburnians live forever.

Unholy Water is a dark and bloodthirsty novel about desire in wild excess, about whether you should defy your circumstances or adapt to them, and about the kind of inflexible determination that can save or destroy those that matter most.

Available in Paperback and for Kindle.

Emerald Wren and the Coven of Seven
By J.J. Barnes

    As a child, Emerald's grandfather gives her a magic lamp with the promise that she can change the world. As an adult Emerald is working hard as a waitress by day, and as part of a crime fighting coven by night.
    And when they get news of a man working his way across the country, burning women to death in his wake, Emerald's coven of seven must take on the biggest challenge of their lives, and risk everything to save the people they love.
    Available in Paperback and for Kindle.

Printed in Great Britain
by Amazon